# SO, YOU THOUGHT GOLF WAS EASY

*By*

*DAVID PENDLEBURY*

# Dedication

To all the friends I have had the pleasure of golfing with over the years in Fenelon Falls, Alliston, The Villages, and other golf venues.

To my sons, of whom I am very proud and who are the inspiration for this novel.

And especially to my wife and partner, Margaret.

# About the Author

I was born in Windsor, Ontario, and attended Assumption High School and the University of Western Ontario, where I graduated with a degree in Physical Education.

I lived in Fenelon Falls, Ontario, for many years, which I still consider home, and presently, I reside in Alliston, Ontario. Due to my checkered background, friends have called me a Renaissance man.

I was a founder of a cable television network called Cable Cable, which provides television and internet services in central Ontario. I coached various championship sports teams at the secondary school and community levels. I participated in many sports, of which golf was my favorite.

I was a mountain climber who, for a few years, was in the Rocky Mountain Rescue Service. I have appeared in several television shows, commercials, and National Geographic Magazine.

# Table of Contents

# Introduction

The young Michigander was living an idyllic life, a near-perfect dream. Each day seemed to unfold as his life story was unblemished by realities that were concealed over time. Unaware of the whims of fate, he would get through his youthful days relatively unburdened. The young man was oblivious to what destiny held in store for him.

With time, he would eventually come to confront his biggest nightmare. He was blissfully unaware of what was to follow in his life. The pendulum of life would lead him to soar to heights only to plunge him into the depths of desolation. He would experience a swing in his life that would be unimaginable for most people!

The grown young man would have an affair with a beautiful, recently separated young woman. More time would pass, and while he was in his early twenties, he would be stalked by an attractive, deranged young female. This young lady would shadow his every move. This woman became so obsessed and infatuated with the young man that Garney would live in fear for both his and his family's lives. During this horrible period of his life, he could only try to recall a simpler and safer past.

As the next few years unfurled, he would find himself in a labyrinth, his spirit alive with measures of hope and with equal trepidation. For now, however, the young Michigander remained cocooned in the blissful ignorance of the rocky road ahead. Let us join him in his unique and disturbing tale.

# Chapter 1: Garney

Everything was dark and very still on that typically brisk spring night. It was a little past three a.m. on Michigan's lower peninsula. Young Garney stirred, and his tortoise-shelled cat meowed with a mild protest. The young man's bed was the only one in the Foster household where the family cat was allowed to seek refuge during the night. When it was still a kitten, the teenager's mother, Maggie, had adopted the pet from the local animal rescue center. Before long, the cat was named Wedge and had become Garney's pet.

Garney suddenly bolted upright. Rolling over, he leaned on his elbows and peered at his alarm clock. He quickly realized the digital clock with oversized numbers was flashing *'12 o'clock.'*

The bond between Garney and Wedge had grown stronger over the years; they became inseparable companions. As Garney bolted upright, he could see the faint silhouette of his feline friend gazing at him with curious eyes.

"Damn storms, the efin power went out again! Shit! I'm gonna be late!"

Electric outages have become a common occurrence in this area of Michigan, particularly at this time of the year. Electrical storms have become a regular occurrence during the spring season of every year. The seventeen-year-old quickly reached for his

1

eyeglasses, which were placed on the night table on the right side of his bed. While feeling for his glasses, he brushed his alarm clock to the floor. As he swung his legs from the bed, his left foot brushed against Wedgy. The crashing sound of the alarm clock hitting the floor and his master's foot found his cat scurrying from her resting place at the foot of Garney's bed.

"Shit," he whispered as he flicked on his bedside lamp. "Sorry, Wedge, I gotta find out what time it is." Shielding his eyes, Garney hurriedly exited his bedroom, wearing only his white undershorts. He moved rapidly along the upper hall, slipped down the stairs, and walked quickly along a lower corridor toward the rear of the house.

Upon entering the family kitchen, he flicked on the overhead ceiling lights. Squinting again, with his hand shading his eyes, he was quite relieved to see the battery-operated wall clock situated over the microwave was showing 3:10. All of the appliance clocks were flashing 12:00 o'clock. He debated whether he should take the time to reset the clocks. It was a little task he liked to do to see if he could synchronize them to read precisely the same time. He wanted things, to be precise; it was his nature that he preferred accuracy. Due to the time of night, he deferred the chore of synchronizing the flashing timepieces. On that early morning, Garney was attempting to be particularly quiet. He was accidentally up and about a little earlier than his recent rising times. His mother had cautioned him that she had only one condition. If he were allowed to accept the job offer at their private golf club, it would depend on him not waking any other family member. He was also aware that since he was awake, if he were to begin his work a little earlier, he could finish a bit earlier. This would allow some extra time in the study hall to prepare for that day's science quiz. His father had also imposed a condition on him. He had to maintain a 3.0 grade point average. This was his father Steven's ultimatum for Garney to be able to accept a job at the Birch Run Golf and Country Club.

Garney Foster slid into the bench seat of the family breakfast nook and gazed over the rear yard and its empty flower bed gardens. He was once again eagerly anticipating the morning ahead. It was still quite dark, and he could just barely make out the outline of the trees at the rear of their property. The white utility shed, which housed the garden tools, the hoses, and a green riding lawn mower, was all that was barely visible. Mowing their large lawn on the family lawn tractor had become his favorite chore. He could immediately see the results of his efforts. Garney had often crosscut the lawn to give it a fairway-like appearance. The immediacy of results and precision were two of Garney's traits.

Garney fixed a quick breakfast consisting of a large glass of orange juice and two pieces of leftover cold pizza. This wouldn't have impressed his mother or his older brother, Bo. They would each be concerned for different reasons, and neither would have been impressed. For his mother, Maggie, it was all about nutrition. The first meal of the day, according to Maggie, was the most important meal of the day.

Everybody, except for his mother, called his brother, Robert or Bob, by his nickname "Bo." This particular cold pizza was some leftover pizza that belonged to Bo. After the previous evening's baseball or track practice, he returned home with some leftover slices. Some team sport always seemed to be in season for Bo. Garney was a junior, and Bo was a senior at the local Grayling High School. Steve, their eldest brother, had graduated from the local high school and was now a sophomore at Bowling Green State University in the neighboring state of Ohio. He was in attendance at the university on a full-ride hockey scholarship – all expenses paid. He wore the colors of Brown and Orange of the Bowling Green Falcons hockey team. A little-known fact was once explained to Garney by his oldest brother. When the Cleveland Browns of the National Football League began their NFL franchise, they needed to request permission from Bowling Green State University to adopt and use the colors Brown and Orange.

After he finished eating what had passed for breakfast, he slid out of his seat and left the nook and the kitchen. He retraced his steps upstairs to his bedroom. A face cloth, a hairbrush, a toothbrush, and deodorant soon followed what had passed for his first meal of the day. Hopefully, after work, there would still be time to shower in the boy's locker room at the high school. This would still leave him enough time to prepare for that day's science test in the study hall before his classes began. His grade point average was well above his father's requirements. He didn't want to take any chances of having to leave his new position at the golf club due to poor grades.

The high school fall football and spring track coach, Mr. Birk, was also his grade eleven science teacher. Garney had declined to sign up for track practices. He knew coach Birk would try to recruit him for the school's spring track team. The sprint team was Mr. Birk's pride and joy. His 4x4 track teams had medaled for six years and been state champions twice. Garney's opting not to join the track team weighed on him as he knew Coach Birk was disappointed. The coach had always admired the Foster boys' natural athleticism and repeatedly encouraged him to run for the school track team that spring. Garney had a clear vision of his priorities. He knew balancing his new job, his studies, and adding an extracurricular activity would be highly challenging.

# Chapter 2: Birch Run Country Club

Garney dressed hurriedly and returned to the kitchen. He patted Wedgy, who had followed his every step, down and up and down again on the stairs in the Foster home. Then, perhaps out of spite, he tore off a piece of Bo's pizza and placed it in the cat's dish. The teen wondered, "Why did I do that?" Deep down inside, he knew he was trying to get even with Bo, who coveted his cold pizza.

His brother Bo had attempted to persuade their parents not to allow Garney to accept his job with Mr. Trent at the local country club. Bo had argued against him working at the golf course for purely selfish reasons. On most school days, the family's second vehicle had been Bo's to drive back and forth to his classes at the high school. Under the new arrangement, Garney drove the vehicle first to his new job at the country club and then, after he finished work, on to the high school. At the onset, his parents seemed a little apprehensive about this compromise. Garney had received his permanent driving license just a few months before this new driving arrangement. Now, begrudgingly, Bo rode the yellow school bus to his classes at Grayling High School. Bo then had to find his younger brother to retrieve the car keys before school classes ended each day. On most days, Bo usually had a game or practice to attend after his classes. Garney played his own game recently. He would try to avoid being seen by Bo at school for as long as possible. Just to have Bo worry a little. Brotherly love.

6

Days passed, and the tension between Garney and Bo not only lingered but also grew. The brothers had always been close, but this recent clash was causing a rift between them. Garney couldn't understand why Bo was so strongly against his new job. It was only for the balance of the school year until the summer vacation arrived.

# Chapter 3: The Drive

Garney picked up his Kodiak work boots and removed the car keys from a hook, which hung near the kitchen door. He quietly closed the kitchen door and moved through the darkness along the driveway towards the white Chevrolet Blazer. The white vehicle was only two years old, and the side doors were emblazoned in large red and yellow font with the family business name, 'Foster's Hardware.' The logo 'Nobody is Faster than Foster' was lettered in smaller print just beneath the company name. Garney wondered whose corny idea had come up with that logo. He almost disliked the slogan more than he disliked his name. "Garney!" Only his mother always called him Garnet. What kind of name was that to attach to a boy? Steve and Robert were the boys' names. Could his mom and dad not find a book of names? Did they run out of relatives that they liked? Garney had always believed children should be allowed to name themselves at age six when they began elementary school. Until then, they could be numbered or lettered in their birth order. He would have been called "three" or "C" during his formative years. Nevertheless, Garney was willing to begrudgingly concede that his parent's choice of Garney did fit somewhat, as this given name rhymed with one of his idols, Arnie.

As Garney settled into the driver's seat, he felt a strange mix of emotions. The engine rumbled to life, and the soft glow of the dashboard illuminated his thoughtful expression. He turned the

Blazer, the headlights cutting through the darkness as he navigated the familiar route to the country club. He recalled the moments of friction with Bo, the tense arguments about the car, and their growing apart. Garney determined he should talk to Bo to clear the air, as they were once best of friends.

Jet black inky darkness was changing to a slightly lesser black as he drove the seven miles to the Birch Run country club. Garney's mind was dancing as quickly as the stars that were starting to appear above. It was one of his traits; his mind was always in motion. A spring weather front was moving east and slowly beginning to reveal a clearer sky above this area of Michigan. The white family truck ran smoothly, and the white highway lines raced toward him as if the highway was in motion.

It was one of those nights when the stars began to shine, but without the assistance of the moon, they had little effect in illuminating the surroundings. He wondered if his father was still disappointed that he hadn't pursued team sports as relentlessly as his brothers. Garney had as much natural athletic ability as his eldest brother, Steve, and nearly as much as Bo. Perhaps he was just imagining what his father's thoughts were. Until recently, he had participated in the same activities as his siblings had participated in before him. His interests changed and evolved over these past two years. Garney's first love was now the game of golf.

As he neared his destination, lost in his thoughts, he recalled the quiet beauty of the well-maintained golf club grounds, which filled him with a sense of calm.

# Chapter 4: Stephan Senior

The boys' mother, Maggie Foster, had been a fine local amateur golfer. She regularly played on Tuesday mornings at the country club in the ladies' eighteen-hole golf league, which occurred during the spring, summer, and fall golf seasons. When the boys were relatively young, Maggie had been the ladies' club champion for three years in a row. For the past several years, during the summer months, his mother and father usually played 18 holes of golf at their club on Sunday afternoons.

There were seven other couples in the "golf group." Anne and Harold Grant were his parents' regular playing partners and their best friends. The Grants were owner-operators of one of the local automobile dealerships in Grayling. Dinner for the group usually followed their Sunday afternoon golf game in the club dining room. The men discussed the shots of their afternoon golf game while the ladies talked about their families and the upcoming social events. The ladies' golf game was in the past and no longer as important as it was for their spouses. The men discussed many of each other's shots they played that afternoon.

The boys' father, Stephen Senior, was affectionately known by his nickname "Swamp." All his friends, neighbors, and the customers of their family hardware store referred to him by his nickname. While in his youth, like his sons who followed him, their father had participated in most of the popular team sports. Swamp attended Michigan Tech University, located on the state's upper peninsula, during his university years. He had attended the university on a full hockey scholarship. Stephen Senior occasionally mentioned that for two years when he was at university in Houghton, Michigan, Tony Esposito, who had an illustrious career in the NHL, was their team goaltender. Swamp was still involved with the local old-timer hockey team called the "Grayling Antiques." During the winter months, Stephen Senior always looked forward to his Wednesday night pickup games and the occasional weekend old-timer's tournaments. These tournaments were usually held in their state and the adjacent province of Ontario in Canada.

Twice over the past few years, their Antiques team had traveled to California to participate in Charles Schulz of *Peanut's renown,* famous hockey tournament. The Snoopy tournament had hosted senior old-timer teams from throughout North America for what seemed to be generations.

Garney's father was raised the son of a fairly wealthy family in Grosse Pointe Woods, which is located in an exclusive suburb in the city of Detroit. The city of Detroit is also better known as the 'motor city.' Garney's paternal grandparents were second-generation owners and operators of a prosperous automobile parts manufacturing company. Swamp's older brother and sister remained in Detroit and owned and managed what was now a third-generation family business. The Foster family was well-connected and long-time members of the prestigious Loch Moor Country Club and the

Grosse Pointe Yacht Club. The family traveled in most of Grosse Pointe's prominent social circles. Garney's grandparents had always hated his father's nickname. They, with their favorite daughter-in-law Maggie, were the only people who always referred to his father as Stephen.

Garney's brother, Stephen Junior, much to his eldest brother's dismay and efforts, had never acquired a nickname. In the long run, his brother was probably fortunate. Somehow, to Garney, the name "Swamp" did not befit the man he admired and respected.

# Chapter 5: Team Sports

Garney's mind quickly changed gears at a "T" in the road, almost synchronizing with the Chevy Blazer's transmission. Why would his father name his first-born son Stephen? Surely, he must have been aware of the teasing he had lived with as a young man. The teasing followed Stephen Junior as it had his father before him – Stephen Foster. "Write us an efin song, Stevie," was a chant often heard from his friends and opponents while in his high school years. Much to their opponent's dismay, it usually spurred the young Foster athlete on to greater efforts.

The younger Steven had attempted to have others call him Junior, but to no avail. The self-assigned nickname just did not seem to suit him. Garney remembers his father telling him that the name Swamp came from the noted music composer's tune 'Suwannee River.' As much as he disliked the nickname and the opponents using it, Garney's father said he preferred it to the teasing he received from his peers. His father believed if he ignored his nickname, it would just go away, but 'Swamp' remains still to this day.

Garney and his brothers had always appreciated the fact that their father had never tried to relive his youth through their activities. Both of their parents had always attended the boys' games and supported their teams. Not once had they ever embarrassed any of their sons during their games, unlike some of the other players' parents. On the contrary, they encouraged and cheered. Unlike some parents, they never interfered with their son's coaches, the opposition, or the officials.

The Foster family hardware business had always been an excellent corporate citizen. The business was one of the best merchant sponsors of the youth teams in the community. You could always depend on Foster's Hardware to step up and provide team uniforms and equipment for aspiring young athletes in the community. Garney, the youngest Foster, had been involved in all the traditional adult-organized activities that revolved around team sports. The seasonal sports such as baseball, hockey, and soccer teams were where you could find all of the Foster brothers during their youth.

Presently, Garney preferred to participate in a sport where he alone was the primary factor in the outcome. No coaches nor teammates to rely on, no one to blame or share in a victory or a defeat. He was the only person dependent on his success or his failure. He now preferred the game of golf. It was an activity where honor and integrity were more important than wins or losses. Players called penalties on themselves for the most minor rule violations or infractions. Garney had enjoyed tennis as a youngster but had lost interest as more tennis role models began to display tempestuous, childish behavior. Breaking racquets was still the norm among many professionals. There did not seem to be a sportsman like Bjorn Borg playing tennis anymore. Too many young players were emulating

Conners and McEnroe. Too many of the imitator-like players were participating in the game.

During his last two school years, Garney had disappointed various high school coaches season after season. He had chosen not to attend tryouts for the different high school teams. He had the highest ability scores in the skills tests in his physical education classes. His brothers had been leaders on the various teams that they had participated in before Garney. During his sophomore high school year, he opted to spend his free time on the one activity that meant the most to him. With every bit of available time, he could be found at the country club practicing or playing the game of golf. He would often ride his bicycle from high school or from home to play or practice at his parent's country club. He was able to fit in some time at the golf course on school days after classes and before dinner. It was at the country club where Garney first met the club's head professional, Mr. George Trent.

The previous fall, the high school football coach had lamented to those who would listen that the regional football championship was probably out of reach. Garney Foster had chosen not to participate in the high school football league for the Grayling school team.

The coach often stated, "Could you imagine two faster Fosters, Bo and Garney, in the same backfield." Coach Birk had cajoled, had private talks with Garney, and even telephoned Maggie and Swamp to try to solicit their support. Coach Birk had asked team members and Garney's peers to encourage him to join the team. Unfortunately, all attempts to change the youngest Foster lad's mind had failed to budge the talented young man from his decision. He would much rather spend his time playing or practicing golf.

# Chapter 6: Mr. Trent

Garney was nearing his destination, and the first hints of dawn started to appear. As he made a left turn to enter the laneway, the small truck's headlights brushed, one by one, past a row of stately pines standing to the right of the entrance road.

He drove by a large, elaborate wooden sign carved with 'Birch Run Golf and Country Club' lettering. The sign picturing white birch trees and the white painted lettering marked the entrance to the driveway. He was twenty minutes earlier than his usual arrival time. He would soon be disappointed to see Mr. Trent's new red Cadillac Seville standing in the head professional's reserved parking spot. Garney had hoped to impress his friend and his mentor by opening the storage garage and begin preparing the day's equipment. The garage lights were already on, and activity had begun. Routine preparation was underway at the Birch Run course for another early spring golf day.

"Good morning, Mr. Trent," Garney exclaimed as he entered the storage garage.

"Good morning, Garney. I have asked you, please just call me George."

"Last night's paper said there would be no rain today, and temperatures will be in the upper sixties—sixty-eight, I think, Mr. Trent."

George Trent sighed; the young man couldn't bring himself to refer to an adult by their first name—a sign of his upbringing, George supposed.

"Yep, this is a great stretch of weather for this early in the season. It makes a lot of golfers happy," he replied.

George Trent was tall, graying, distinguished, and quite tanned due to another winter in central Florida. He had returned to Michigan once again in early April. George had followed the sun most of his adult years. The one concession he had made to the sun's rays was his familiar wide-brimmed hat. A physician had warned the head professional about the diminishing ozone layer and an increased hazard of skin cancer. He had been warned long before the concern was widely known. The doctor had advised George to wear a hat with a brim, definitely not a baseball-type cap. The doctor had seen skin cancer on the top of some of his golfer patient's ears. His hat almost seemed to be part of his features. People thought George must have owned hundreds of wide-brimmed hats because his hats always seemed so new and clean. The one exception was when George was working in the storage garage. He wore his old, battered favorite hat, which he hung on a hook near the storage door entrance.

Garney finished lacing up his work boots and began his chores without receiving any instructions or directions from his mentor. After two weeks, he knew the routine, loved where he was, and loved what he was doing.

Before too long, other vehicles began to cast their headlights up the driveway entrance; two pickup trucks and an older model Ford Tempo, which had seen better days, were moving in single file up the laneway. They were soon lined up in the staff parking lot alongside the Foster family Blazer and George's Cadillac. Lights and engines were extinguished. Soon, five men were working alongside Garney in preparation for the golf day ahead. The light of dawn was beginning to emerge, and before long, a small army of golf carts left the storage area in single file. The worker's golf carts began scattering in several directions to prepare the golf course for play that day. There was morning dew to be removed from the greens, traps to be raked, flag pin placements changed, sprinkler heads checked, drinking water containers replaced by fresh, full, icy cold ones, and waste basket contents to be emptied from the previous day. These tasks and a few others had to be completed, and the golf course had to be prepared for members' play before the first scheduled tee-off time at *7:15 a.m.* You could see the lights in the pro shop as the club's assistant pro opened the shop's check-in counter for business. Mister Trent had departed toward the member's golf club storage shed to unlock the building and turn on the lights.

Each worker's cart left railroad-like tracks on the wet grass as they dispersed in various directions. Garney was never happier as he drove his maintenance cart in the direction of the fifteenth tee box.

The back of the cart was loaded with all the equipment that would be required for his morning duties. While driving, he clipped a computer printout to the steering wheel – the printout located that day's flag pin placements on the greens. While en route, the young employee noticed a leaking sprinkler head, causing a small pond of water to form. Garney mentally noted the problem while driving across the tenth fairway. This was not an area assigned to him, but he would place the information on the daily morning report that the greens keepers turned in after their duties each morning. There were occasional day breaks when one could observe some of the area's wildlife on the golf course. Only two mornings prior, he had witnessed three deer crossing a fairway. He could never understand how his father and two brothers looked forward to the fall deer hunting season. He could never bring himself to hunt deer. The beauty of a golf course and all its creatures were a significant part of the reason for his love of the game.

On this particular day, Garney was assigned to the fifteenth through eighteenth holes as his responsibility. Due to the elevation changes, they were his four favorite holes on the golf course. The sixteenth was the signature hole for the Birch Run golf course. It was a downhill par three fronted by a pond.

Garney worked in his usual efficient and thorough manner. A complete course grooming would be attended to during the daytime playing hours throughout the week. Fairways would be mowed, and the rough would be trimmed by the full-time staff, each in white golf shirts, green slacks,and green baseball caps. The time passed quickly, and before long, he left his final designated 18th green to return toward the storage area.

As he drove past the main parking lot, he could see some early morning golfing arrivals. Three late-model cars stood in their marked spaces in the parking lot. A few club members were strolling in the direction of the locker room. Golfers are a passionate part of the human race, often rising in the early morning to play their game. One of the individuals seemed to be showing his colleagues a new golf club. New equipment kept the game alive for many golfers. Amateur players were constantly looking for the magic wand, that new training device, a longer playing ball, or the more forgiving golf club. Golfers purchased any new product that they believed could lower their scores. Brand name and imitation knock-off manufacturers and suppliers raced to place new golf products on the market each spring. Golf game equipment was constantly changing. Titanium, adjustable, and bigger drivers seemed to be the rage these last few years. There were golf clubs that included an adjustable wrench, which players could use to customize the club for different lofts and shot shapes before their game. Golf had become a multi-billion-dollar business. Garney always kept senior pro golfer Lee Trevino in mind when he had the urge to look at the newest golf club. Mr. Trevino often stated that it wasn't the arrow but the Indian.

# Chapter 7: The Morning Duties

The final morning task was underway, and he began to assist the other workers in moving the battery-operated rental golf carts to their parking area. The golf carts were checked for a full electric charge and then unplugged from their charging stations. They ensured each cart contained a rake for repairing the player's imprints in the sand traps, two full containers of a sand seed mixture for repairing divots, and a golf scorecard with a club logo pencil clipped to the steering wheel. Garney always tried to align the rental carts as if they were a proud drill team waiting for their daily instruction.

As he had previously planned, his work was finished early. Now, he debated whether he should assist in removing the dew from the practice putting green or depart for school to prepare for his upcoming science test. Recalling his father's admonition, "Keep up your grades," he removed his work boots. He kept a spare pair of Nike sports shoes in the family car to wear at school these last few days. Garney turned in his computer printout with some notes, remembering to indicate the sprinkler head he had observed malfunctioning earlier.

He eased the family vehicle back down the entrance driveway, which he had navigated three hours earlier in the opposite direction.

Garney knew that summer would soon be here, and he would be able to spend entire days at the golf club where he was the happiest. It was now more daylight than dawn, and the best part of his day was behind him. Imagine that he received a wage and golfing privileges for doing something he would do for free!

# Chapter 8: Maggie

Later that same afternoon, Maggie was busying herself with some of her daily routines, and Wedgy moved from room to room following her. The cat, an adopted stray four years ago, had become one of the family. Her husband initially had refused to consider having another pet after their family dog had been euthanized five years earlier. The drive to the veterinary clinic was almost more than Stephen Senior could bear. Stephen and his dog were not unlike George and his wide-brimmed hats. The dog was like a part of his features. Stephen and Duffy in the truck, Stephen and Duffy in the store, Stephen and Duffy in the yard; they would always be together. For years, you never seemed to see one without the other.

Maggie had supported and sided with Garney on the adoption of Wedge, who became the newest resident in their home. From the beginning, only she and Garney seemed to give Wedge any care and attention. What a silly name, she had always thought. Her youngest son, then thirteen, insisted that the cat be called Wedge, named after the smallest golf club in his golf bag. His brothers and father had a different locker room version of a wedgy and initially had some fun with the cat's name. Garney continued to be responsible for the care of Wedge long after the family pet had become a novelty. Wedgy would hear the sound of the approaching yellow school bus long before it loomed into sight each school day. The cat persisted in being let outside to greet her friend and master.

25

Maggie's parents and siblings, two sisters and a brother, continued to live in Frankenmuth, Michigan, where she had been raised. Frankenmuth is a Bavarian-style community famous for Christmas decorations, chicken dinners, and a vast nearby outlet mall, ironically named "Birch Run." She missed being closer to her family and managed a few trips yearly to Frankenmuth on the pretense of shopping for clothes or gifts. The trip was a drive of one hundred and twenty miles one way and lasted just over two hours on Interstate Highway 75. She and Stephen always arranged a visit to her home neighborhood every autumn. They loved to visit her family's home to attend the Frankenmuth Octoberfest each fall.

Maggie had met Stephen during their college years in northern Michigan. She was a friend of one of his hockey teammates. When they were first introduced, she had a crush on Stephen long before he knew of her interest in him. Margaret May Hausen was aware that males were sometimes slow to recognize an infatuation during their maturing years. She believed at this stage, most males were more preoccupied with bedding the opposite sex than having a social relationship with them. Maggie and Stephen had dated, courted, married, and still loved each other very much. Their life was wholesome. Their hardware business was very successful. Three sons of whom they were very proud made their life nearly complete. Maggie had secretly longed for a possible granddaughter someday in the future. Their eldest son, Steve, was attending Bowling Green University on a hockey scholarship in the neighboring state of Ohio.

Steve worked in the family hardware store between semesters and when he was home during the summer months. He had returned two weeks ago after completing his second year of studies. Steven had a long-range ambition to enter law school.

The middle child, Bo, was completing his final year at the local high school. He would attend the University of Michigan the next fall on a football scholarship. However, even though he was finishing high school, he had no idea what academic direction, if any, he wished to pursue. This was an ongoing concern for his parents, Maggie and Stephen.

During the early years of their marriage, Maggie frequently anticipated the arrival of a new member to the family. She secretly desired a daughter, but complications with the birth of Garnet prevented their plans of having any more children. Perhaps having three children in five years had taken a physical toll. Even though she and Stephen had tried for a daughter, Maggie would never get pregnant again.

# Chapter 9: The Disappointment

Suddenly, Wedge left her side and trotted to the kitchen door, a sure sign that the yellow school bus would soon be visible at the end of the driveway. Maggie opened the door, and the cat dashed out and down the driveway for her usual greeting. Garney usually carried a small treat for his pet in his pocket.

Maggie began to brace herself for Garnet's description of that morning's events. She had promised Stephen that she would talk with their youngest son when he arrived home from school that afternoon. Maggie knew he was going to be met with huge disappointment. Garnet loved his new job at Birch Run. His new position was all he talked about at the dinner table each evening, much to the chagrin of the rest of the family. But plans do change. Bo had to report to Ann Arbor, the home of the Michigan Wolverines, for fitness and weight training sessions to prepare for the upcoming football season. Stephen now needed their youngest son to work in the hardware store during the summer to replace Bo. The boys had always worked at the hardware store part-time during the school year and full-time during the summer months. Bo, in particular, loved working in the family store. The sons were dependable workers who were much like assistant managers for their father. Bo's early departure to the Michigan campus would require Garnet to replace him at the family store during the upcoming summer months. Garney would have to leave his job at the country club. Instead of Stephen Junior and Bo working at the store this summer, it would have to be Garney and his older brother Stephen assisting their father in the family store.

The side door swung open, and the young man and his cat entered the kitchen. Maggie was busy with her dinner preparation. She knew she had to begin with the disappointing news immediately. She had a promise to keep to her husband. Letting the moment slide would make it difficult to muster up the courage again before Stephen Senior arrived home from the store.

"Sit down, Garnet. Would you like an apple?"

Garney immediately knew that something was imminent. His mother always offered a piece of fruit, some cookies, or a sandwich when she had something serious to discuss. Her husband often teased her that she liked to fatten the lamb for the slaughter.

"No thanks, mom. What's up?"

After ten minutes of discussion, Garney was crestfallen. His mind whirled. There had to be a way out of this mess. For the first time, he hated that the Fosters owned a family business. Why couldn't his father work for someone else like other fathers? Why did Bo have to accept the football scholarship? Bo had also been offered a hockey scholarship at Michigan State in Lansing, and hockey players didn't have to report that early in the summer. He thought there had to be some possible way around his devastating problem.

Later that evening, assistance arrived from an unexpected source – a source that nobody could have anticipated. Bo sensed the massive disappointment that his brother Garney was facing and how down he was probably feeling. Bo wanted to do something to help, even though he and Garney were not particularly close recently. Bo suggested that he might be able to receive special permission from his football coach or the athletic director and the Michigan football coaching staff. It would allow him to do some of his pre-season training during the month of July in his hometown.

Permission was occasionally granted by the coaching staff in Ann Arbor to enable football athletes to train at theirlocal facilities. The local Grayling High School exercise rooms were available in the evenings for weight training. He still had to report for the opening of training camp at the Wolverine campus during the first week of August. This would give his father some time to devise a possible solution. Garney would be able to work at the golf club for at least part of this summer's season. Maggie and Stephen agreed and felt very proud of Bob's consideration for his brother. Bo wouldn't admit this possible change prevented him from leaving his home for another month. He was a homebody. Bo never had to hunt for Garney and the car keys for the remainder of the school year.

# Chapter 10: Michigan Golf

It was a wonderfully memorable season for the rest of that summer. One of Bo's classmates, the son of one of his father's best friends, began to work at Foster's hardware store in early June. He was competent, and the store's operation never lost a beat. Bo as was scheduled, left for Ann Arbor in late July, and even Garney missed his presence around the house. They had spent some time golfing together when Garney had finished his daily work. When he left for work, Garney would take Bo's golf clubs and a change of clothes for his brother in the light truck. Bo would jog the five miles to Birch Run after he had finished his workday at the hardware store. The arrangement was excellent for Bo's conditioning but didn't do much for his ego. Garney had developed into a fine young junior golfer and now played with a four handicap. Golf was the only game that Bo could not compete on an equal basis with his youngest brother. Bo had always been a decent golfer. However, over the last two years, Garney's diligence and love for the game have developed him into an exceptional young golfer. Bo's high eighty and low ninety scores fell well short of Garney's low to mid-seventies results. Bo often offered that he had just jogged five miles as a reason for the difference in their scores, and this had given Garney an unfair advantage.

Mr. Trent's golf instructions had begun to polish and refine Garney's game to a point where he had developed a reputation in amateur junior golf circles in the state.

This area of Michigan had gained its reputation for being called the 'Myrtle Beach of the North.' The site had become known as the 'Golf Mecca of Michigan.' Boyne Mountain, Grand Traverse, Michaywe in Gaylord, and Marsh Ridge were some of the excellent golf vacations and destinations for golfers from both the United States and the neighboring Canadian province of Ontario. New golf courses were in the planning stages, were being built, and were being opened for play. These newer courses only added to the area's many fine existing golf facilities. The youngest Foster dreamed of someday becoming a golf club professional. He wanted to be like his mentor, Mr. Trent.

After his working hours at the club, Garney received some personal instruction one or two times a week from his mentor. With these private lessons, Garnet spent innumerable hours on his own, every free moment practicing his golf game. The practice facility at the golf club took a beating that summer. The driving range, the putting green, and the practice sand traps were like a second home to the teenager in his free time.

Garney had become what was known as a golf purist. He always walked and always carried his golf bag. He never used a mulligan nor winter rules, even when the conditions permitted.

Garney was meticulous when filling in his scorecard, ensuring that he entered an accurate score. Garney also kept personal golf statistics on his scorecard. He wrote down his number of putts, his greens in regulation, and the fairways he hit during each round of golf. He wanted to know where he needed the most improvement and some additional work. It sometimes irked Bo when he used a mulligan from the tee that Garney would state "should be three off the tee." Garney had scored below par for the first time that summer. On three separate occasions, he had achieved scores of seventy-one on the par seventy-two course. Once, due to some excellent putting, he had scored sixty-nine. The sixty-nine was only six strokes higher than Mr. Trent's course record of sixty-three.

During that season, the young man continued to improve, and he gained respect from his tutor and the friendship of the staff and the country club members. Several life-changing events were going to occur to him that summer!

# **Chapter 11: Caddying**

On one special occasion, Mr. Trent asked Garney to caddie for him in a local club professional tournament. This tournament was hosted by the Grand Traverse Resort in Traverse, Michigan. It was a tournament for the golf pros who were working professionals and not touring professionals. The tournament took place over two days. The first round was played at 'The Bear,' a Jack Nicklaus-designed course regarded as the top golf facility in the region. George and Garney commuted back to Grayling after the first day of play. The next and final day of play resumed at Spruce Run, which had often hosted the state's championship tournament.

There were several tournaments for the club professionals each summer, and George Trent usually entered two or three of these events. Ben Atkinson, the most senior employee and head greens keeper at the Birch Run facility, usually served as George's caddie in these events. Ben had caddied for George for as long as anyone could remember.

On this particular occasion, Ben had suggested to George, "Take Garney to this tournament; he'll enjoy it." The head greenskeeper was fond of Garney and his work ethic. He had never had a young employee so dependable and who took such pride in his work. Ben would miss going on the golf trip but saw such promise in the young individual that he willingly made the sacrifice. For a few days before the tournament, Ben spent some time with Garney, explaining the nuances of caddying. Knowing where to stand, when to attend the pin, when to have the correct club ready for the player, and counting the clubs in the golf bag before starting the round was essential. The player didn't need penalties or a disqualification to ruin his day.

After two days of play, George had finished ninth in the tournament and was relatively satisfied with his game. Due to the demands at his country club, like many other club professionals, he played less golf than he would have liked. Operating the pro shop, giving lessons, organizing his staff, and organizing club members and their tournaments tended to limit the amount of time to play golf for many of the club professionals.

George was impressed and proud of Garney's insight for tournament play. His protege always offered him the proper club and even assisted him in reading the lines of his putts. Garney took his responsibilities of caddying very seriously and had an excellent understanding of the game. The young caddie loved the atmosphere, the camaraderie, the treatment the players received, and being so close to the action. The two-day tournament was over too soon. During the fifty-mile trip home after the tournament ended, Mr. Trent allowed Garney to drive his prized red Cadillac Seville. George was able to doze during the drive home. That tournament was almost the best time of the summer!

# Chapter 12: Dave Patterson

Encouraged by Mr. Trent, Garney had entered several amateur tournaments in the state and had played very well. In some tournaments, he competed with his peers in age-level competitions. In other tournaments, he competed with seasoned adult amateurs. After all of his events, a fifth-place finish was his best placing, and compliments were given to him on his ability and composure. In some instances, organizers and fellow competitors, after the round of golf, would offer him guidance on his course play management. Whenever it was possible, Garney's family and Mr. Trent attended his matches to support him. Quietly, their pride was very apparent. Playing in these regional tournaments was almost the best time of that summer.

On Garney's birthday in late July, George invited the young man and his parents to join him for dinner. They were to be his guests at the country club. The Tudor-style 'Run' had one of the better dining rooms in the area. It was rated five stars in the Michigan Tourist Guide. George had a special surprise for the Foster family that evening. When the Foster family arrived, Mr. Trent was seated at the table with another gentleman. As the family approached, both men stood to greet them. Neither Garney nor his parents recognized the stranger who was introduced as George's friend, Dave Patterson. Dave was a friend and colleague from Mr. Trent's competitive years on the PGA tour. During the dinner, it was revealed that Mr.

Patterson was currently the coach and coordinator of the golf program at Western Michigan University in Kalamazoo, Michigan.

Mr. Patterson was there to explore the possibility of Garney attending Western Michigan on a partial golf scholarship after completing his final year of high school. Garney might as well have eaten at a fast-food burger restaurant. Even though the dinner was exquisitely prepared and presented, Garney couldn't remember what he had ordered or what he had consumed. At the conclusion of the dinner, George indicated that he had arranged a golf game the next day for Garney, Mr. Patterson, Ben, and himself. The friendly match was set for nine forty-five the following morning at the club.

# Chapter 13: Get Acquainted

The next morning, Garney, now eighteen, had difficulty eating his breakfast. Mother Maggie expressed her concern as she had always believed that one's first meal of the day was the most important meal of the day. Garney was now a year older, six feet one inch tall, and weighed a little more than one hundred and eighty-five pounds. He was more nervous than he had ever been in his life, with the possible exception of when he saw Carly Brophy at the club. The drive to Birch Run that morning was a blur; before he knew it, he had arrived. He was greeted by Mr. Trent, who called him aside. George recognized Garney's nervousness and assured him that the scholarship offer was not dependent on his play on that particular day. Dave Patterson had quietly attended two of Garney's tournaments that summer and was aware of Garney's ability.

The arrangement was merely so that Mr. Patterson and Garney could get to know each other a little better. Mr. Patterson had based his original scholarship offer on Mr. Trent's initial recommendation and the two earlier tournaments that he had attended.

Their tee time had been arranged to play behind a two-some of local golfers. The two players were club members who knew the course very well, and both were known to play very quickly. This situation would eliminate any delays in play ahead of the 9:45 foursome.

# SO, YOU THOUGHT GOLF WAS EASY

The round of golf began on time. Garney began by playing well below his ability, and he was four over par as they headed for the fifth tee box. After the four tee shots, Ben told a golf story from his extensive repertoire of jokes and anecdotes, which relaxed the young man. Garney began to play better. George had invited Ben to join their foursome for that very reason. The head greenskeeper was always able to put the young Foster at ease.

The joke seemed to do the trick. On his second shot, Garney, on the par five, hit a solid fairway wood from a difficult lie in the rough. The golf ball rose, burrowed through a strong headwind, landed just short of the green, and rolled to within six feet of the flag pin. Garney went on to sink his putt for a two-under-par eagle. Garney played only one more hole over par for the rest of the round and finished with a three over par seventy-five. It was far from his best round, but he had displayed an ability to recover from a poor start. Mr. Trent and Mr. Patterson had a pair of seventy-two rounds, and Ben scored eighty-four. Garney's introduction to the head coach of the Western Michigan University golf team was almost the best time of the summer.

# Chapter 14: Carley Brophy

Garney knew most of the Birch Run Golf and Country Club members on a first-name basis. They always called him Garney, but he always referred to them by their surnames. Mr. This and Mrs. That. He was never comfortable using adults' first names. The very first time Garney saw Carley Brophy, he was struck and enamored by her. He always called her Mrs. Brophy, and she always insisted that he just call her Carley.

Garney had dated occasionally in high school. Dating wasn't as high a priority with him as it was with other teenagers. Garney, who had his family's good looks, was usually approached first by the opposite sex. This social game was one that Garney participated in reluctantly. On Sadie Hawkins's days, his female classmates considered him a 'blue plate special.' The youngest Foster, until this time, had never been sexually active. His dates had ended in kissing and petting, but Garney was still a virgin. He had physical desires, but they were still just below a simmer. Garney was considerably behind most of his teenage peers in the game of romance and sex.

Carley Brophy was brunette, tiny, beautiful, and seductive. She had a way of innocently attracting members of the opposite sex. Carley was nearly twenty-two years old, and she was married. Presently, she had just been separated from her husband after the past New Year's Eve Gala party. Her spouse had left her in January for another woman. Nick Brophy had always resented the attention other men paid to his now estranged wife. The constant arguments and accusations at home after every social event created an acrimony between them. It eventually led to their marriage breaking up. Nick had moved from the Grayling area to live in Shakopee, Minnesota, with his newfound other woman. He still had strong feelings for Carley, but his unfounded jealousy was his breaking point. Carley was faced with new problems now that she was separated and alone. Carley had to constantly rebuff the arduous advances of males, most of whom were married, at the social functions she attended. Men privately referred to her as a tease. Her husband's accusations had been entirely without substance and were completely unfounded. Carley had been married for three years, and now she had ambivalent feelings about her new-found freedom. Carley still loved Nick and, strangely, missed him, but she knew she had to get on with her new life. Initially, arriving alone at social functions made her feel awkward, but she always managed to enjoy herself. Carley was vivacious and often the life of the party. Her real estate sales skills were useful in social settings. The women and the men loved her; they enjoyed her company and always included her on their invitation lists. Women seemed to have a sixth sense about other women who might threaten their relationships, and Carley didn't fall into that category. Even though she found it difficult, Carley always arrived home alone after these social functions. Some married men were often the most challenging and troublesome as she socialized within the community. She had a way of holding a man's arm when talking to him and pressing her ample breast into his biceps during the conversation. She was aware that she was a bit of a tease. Carley was a touching person who often moved into another person's personal space. She had typical female desires, but she kept them on the back burner for now. Mrs. Brophy was at the prime of her sexual life and was a beautiful, charming, and effervescent young woman.

The first week of August brought the start of the men's and ladies' match play championships at the golf club. Carley was well into her match on the fourteenth tee when Garney first saw her that day. She was playing a preliminary match with another lady member, and Carley took the time to give him a wave and a smile. Garney was mowing the men's back tee area at the time with a handheld gas-powered mower.

He stood quietly with the mower, idling until the ladies had hit their tee shots and were about to leave. Carley waved and smiled at him again as the ladies drove off in their golf cart down the cart path toward the fairway.

# Chapter 15: The Meeting

Three hours later, Garney had completed his shift for the day. He was on his way to the golf club storage building when he met Mrs. Brophy again. He had intended to pick up his putter and a few golf balls to spend an hour or so at the practice putting green before leaving for home.

Carley had finished her golf match and had spent time with her opponent in the club lounge. The club lounge was appropriately named 'The End of the Run' and, during the golf season, served light luncheon fare and coffee plus alcoholic and non-alcoholic drinks. Even with her generous USLGA handicap, Carley had lost her match. Among her many attributes, golf was not one of her strong suits. Her opponent that day, Mrs. Lefrance, had driven Carley to the country club that morning. Mrs. Lefrance already had left for her home earlier after they had a coffee in the lounge. Carley indicated to Joan Lefrance that she was going to stay for a late lunch as she was meeting some friends later. Carley had selected a table with a view of everything that was happening around the clubhouse grounds.

Finally, the youngest Foster appeared into view, walking in the general direction of the member's golf club storage shed. He had just returned his lawn mower and other equipment to the cart barns for their use the next day. Carley, in preparation, had previously paid her luncheon tab so that she could quickly leave the lounge area to intercept Garney.

"Hello Garney, I have missed my ride. Could I catch a drive home with you when you leave?" Carley asked as she approached the young man.

"Sure, Mrs. Brophy, I was just going to leave; I go fairly close to your place." Garney was elated to be traveling with her for ten miles, even though the drive was out of his way. He could practice putting tomorrow. Not only was Garney an obliging young man, but this was a beautiful young lady whom he secretly had a crush on.

"Garney, I am playing in a fun tournament at Marsh Ridge in Gaylord this weekend with some lady friends. Would it be possible to put my golf clubs in your trunk? It will save me picking them up tomorrow morning."

"I'll get them now and meet you in the staff parking lot in a few minutes. It's the white Blazer, replied Garney. It's parked near the front row next to Mr. Trent's."

"It would be hard to miss with the hardware logo on the side doors," said Carley as she set off toward the staff parking lot, which was in the opposite direction. Garney was completely unaware that Carley had sat at the lounge window for the past hour, nursing a gin and tonic, awaiting his return from the golf course. Her table had a view of the golf club storage area and the pro shop. She did not want to miss his return from his work on the golf course. Carley had orchestrated this chance meeting. She was quite taken by this handsome and charming young man. Before she spotted him, she had hurried to the ladies' member lounge to freshen up and brush her hair. She was as nervous as if she was readying herself for a first date.

As he continued to the club storage area, Garney could hardly contain his excitement. Garney tried to recall if he had ever been this apprehensive about being around someone of the opposite sex. Mrs. Brophy was certainly memorable. Garney quickly located the proper golf clubs, recalling her golf bag was mauve with matching club head covers. On the way to the Blazer, he stopped to change his shoes in the storage area and briefly talked with Ben about the next day's schedule.

Ben returned to his work on a mower he was repairing when he inquired about Garney's having Mrs. Brophy's golf clubs. After receiving an explanation, Ben jokingly stated, "Now you behave yourself." Garney blushed and replied, "I'm just giving her a ride home."

# Chapter 16: A First Affair

Carley Brophy was standing alongside the Chevy Blazer as Garney arrived. He unlocked the light truck with the keyless handheld remote. Garney then held open the vehicle's passenger door, allowing her to enter, and he apologized for taking so long. Carley slid up into the passenger seat. As he moved to the rear of the vehicle to place her golf clubs in the back compartment, Garney thought her reply was unusual. Mrs. Brophy had stated, "I would wait for you anytime, Garney."

During the drive to her home, the two engaged in pleasant conversation about their golfing. She expressed an interest in his summer, his job, his family, and the tournaments he had participated in during the summer. Garney, in response, inquired about her match that day. Carley, while she was talking, placed her hand on his shoulder several times and once patted his thigh as she commented on her loss in her golf match that day. Garney loved the feeling of her touch, and he blushed continually during the drive. Mrs. Brophy had even stated that she thought he had an interesting name.

As they turned into her driveway, Carley said, "Garney, could you put my golf clubs in the trunk of my car? My car is parked in the garage."

Garney pulled the Blazer to a full stop and turned off the keys in the ignition. Both passengers slid out their respective car doors onto her flower-bed lined, asphalt driveway. Garney retrieved the golf clubs as Carley headed for her house to retrieve the keys to the car and open the automatic garage door. Mrs. Brophy lived on a country sideroad several few miles from town. The house was a beautiful Cape Cod-style bungalow with a double-car attached garage. The home was painted a blue-grey color with white shutters. Her home looked like the front page of a "Better Homes and Gardens" magazine issue. It had several lovely flower gardens and a plush lawn. He wondered how she found time to sell real estate, be active in the community, golf, and maintain her property in such a fine state. The lawn alone was immense and must have required a great deal of attention. Garney carried her golf clubs to the closed garage door and waited for Mrs. Brophy. Carley had entered her home and returned with her car keys to automatically open one of the garage bays. Suddenly, the door began to hum and rise into an open position. Carley reappeared from the back of the garage with her car keys in hand. When the trunk popped open, Garney placed her clubs into the trunk of her midnight blue Lexus. When Carley invited him in for a soda, Garney was beginning to exit the garage door opening. Garney appeared flustered but somehow replied, "Thanks, I could use a soft drink; it was warm out there today."

Mrs. Brophy held the door open, and Garney walked through the side entrance into her home. The large entrance opened to a beautiful kitchen decorated with pale blue and pink pastels. He immediately felt awkward, as he had always held doors open for ladies, and began apologizing for his error of gallantry.

"I'm sorry. I should have held the door for you."

"It's no problem, Garney; I have been used to opening doors for myself this last while."

Garney quickly scanned the areas of the house that he could view from the kitchen area, and he was impressed with the decorating of her home. He suddenly blushed and felt awkward when he realized that he had mentioned opening the door for her. He shouldn't have reminded her, even though inadvertently, about her recent marital situation.

"What a gorgeous home you have, Mrs. Brophy. Do you do your own decorating?"

"Yes, I have always been interested in interior decoration; I hope to open my own consulting business someday. Would you like a Pepsi, or could I make you some lemonade? Have a seat, Garney."

"A Pepsi would be fine, thanks, Mrs. Brophy," Garney replied as he took his place in a chair at the kitchen table. The kitchen windows overlooked a patio pool and a beautifully landscaped backyard. Small herb and vegetable gardens were located at the rear of the yard, which was edged in a variety of flower beds. Two mature fruit trees stood in the center of the property.

Carley placed some ice in a tall glass and then poured the contents of the can of soda over the ice. She asked proudly, "Garney, would you like to see some of the design sketches I have been working on for a friend? They are in the preliminary stage, but they are starting to come together."

"Yes, I'd like to see them," replied Garney.

Carley left the kitchen to retrieve the large folder from another room. While she was gone, Garney couldn't help but think, "How could her husband, Nick, have left such a wonderful, beautiful woman?"

After a few minutes, Carley returned to the kitchen and placed the oversized manila folder in front of Garney on the kitchen table. As he began to browse through her drawings, Carley mixed herself a gin and grapefruit drink. She returned to the table, stood behind the young man, and began explaining some of the various ideas that she had incorporated into her drawings and plans.

Garney was genuinely interested in her drawings. She drew closer to him as the moments passed. Garney could feel her ever-nearing breath on his neck, and soon, her breast gently brushed his shoulder as she reached forward to be able to turn one of the pages of her work. His heart was racing, and he could feel the redness in his face deepen. Their arms were touching, and he hoped the moment could last forever. He gently leaned toward her, and the fullness of her breast pressed against his shoulder as she also leaned into him.

She softly kissed his cheek and turned his face gently toward her. They embraced each other as he drew himself to his feet. As they kissed, they stood together, their bodies pressed against each other.

Carley moved his hand to her breast as she slowly moved her other hand to his groin and began to massage him gently. Incredibly aroused, Carley led Garney from the kitchen area through the living room to the master bedroom. She moved them onto her bed and began to undo his belt. After finding each other for a while and removing their clothes, they made love for what seemed an eternity. Garney made love for the first time in his life, and Carley made love for the first time with someone other than her husband.

While driving home an hour later, Garney's mind was racing. He was alert yet confused, guilty and elated, wanting to see her again, too embarrassed to see her again, wishing it hadn't happened, hoping it would happen again. The whole situation was an enigma, but what a wonderful enigma. Wedge was there to greet him as he stepped out of the Blazer. He picked his pet up and felt safe and relieved. He had returned to his safe world.

# Chapter 17: Nick Returns

The couple had several romantic liaisons as the season continued into the early fall. Garney loved being in her company, but he dreaded their deception and the web of lies he wove to maintain their secrecy. Deep inside, they both knew that the affair had no long-lasting substance. He was responsible and mature but was just entering manhood and his final year of high school. She was a woman who had been married and was gainfully employed, a young, beautiful, mature adult. Only three years older but much more mature as women tend to be.

Late that August, Garney left his home early on a Thursday evening. He had left the house on the pretense of attending a card game at a friend's house. As he drove, he constantly worried about someone seeing the family vehicle en route or while he was turning into Carley's driveway. He was concerned that if the hardware's automobile was seen at Carley's home, his father might be implicated and suspected of being Carley's lover. He made several direction changes on what was becoming a somewhat regular trip. To avoid any possible detection, his irregular route became routine for him. Garney constantly glanced at the faces of oncoming drivers to see if he recognized anyone or if anyone had recognized him.

As he drove, the young man glanced in the rearview mirror as much as he watched the road ahead.

As the vehicle approached the Brophy residence, Garney's emotions began to heighten; his heart was beating faster, and his face was reddening. He had never felt comfortable on these drives, but rather, he felt quite uneasy. Only when in the safety of Carley's residence did he begin to relax and unwind.

When Carley heard his vehicle approach, she went to the garage and pressed the automatic garage door opener to allow Garney to enter and park the Blazer inside. On each arrival, Garney thought the sound of opening the garage door would surely be heard for the entire length of her country road. Carley stood in the doorway to the entrance, and she kissed him gently on the cheek when he arrived.

The relationship was not strictly sexual, although it was essential in caring for each other. During the visits, they generally watched television, talked, and discussed various topics while cuddled on the living room sofa. This particular evening, Carley led him to the kitchen, where they sat opposite each other at the dining table. He remembered he had only been seated at the table once before.

Carley began by saying, "Garney, you know how much I care for you, and the last thing I want to do is hurt you. I am afraid this has to be our final time to be together like this. I think the world of you, but we both know that it is leading to problems for one or both of us. You have an education to think of and a full and happy life ahead of you."

Garney felt saddened and yet relieved, sad, and elated. He acknowledged her and replied somewhat ruefully, "Yes, Carley, I know, but I want you to know this has been wonderful, and I don't just mean making love. Being with you has been special."

"Something else, Garney, I have been talking to Nick on the phone a few times recently, and we will try to get back together in a few weeks. He is moving back home to start over together sometime in late September. We want to try to make a go of our marriage again." Garney quickly responded, "I should go now."

"Yes, that would be best. Please, for my sake, this must continue to be our secret forever. I do care for you, and it was more than just sex for me as well; you are a great person, Garney. I loved our time together. You are going to meet someone someday, when you are older, who will be a fortunate young woman and wants to be with you in a relationship." There was a certain irony to her statement, as time would tell.

"I promise you that I'll never tell a soul, and I am sure that everything will work out between you and Mr. Brophy. Thanks for having me over, and you know everything. I'm happy that you are getting back together."

"I will see you at the country club Garney."

Garney reversed out of his parking spot in the garage and realized for the first time in a few weeks that he felt that he wasn't carrying a burden of guilt. Happy was the most prominent emotion he felt now that Nick Brophy was returning home. Thrilled was more to the point. He knew he would have moments where he still had strong feelings toward Carley, but they both had to move on.

He was now only one more deception from closure to the romance. He wanted to be home and only had to lie to his parents one more time. He even contemplated driving to the golf course and walking around for a few hours. This would allow him to arrive home at a more appropriate time from the card game. He hadn't been gone long enough for his card game excuse.

# Chapter 18: Bo's Accusation

As he slipped down from the 4X4, Wedge was there to greet him. He had only been away for an hour. He picked up his cat and entered through the side door of the house. At the same time, his mother entered the kitchen from the living room. She had heard him arriving home from his card game. Garney quickly blurted out that he had the wrong night for the card game and had come home early because he was a little tired.

Maggie Foster said, "Sit down, Garnet. Would you like some cake?" Garney's heart dropped. He felt certain that his and Carley's indiscretions had been discovered.

"Okay, Mom, I am a little hungry."

He wondered what his mother was going to say. He hoped that it wasn't what he thought it might be. He would only be confronted by his mother by staying in the kitchen and having the cake. It is much easier than being confronted by both parents at once.

As she walked to the refrigerator, Maggie stated, "Your brother Bob is home. A Michigan assistant football coach drove him up from the university and dropped him off while you were gone. He had a knee injury, and football is out for the remainder of this year. He's returning in a few days to resume classes and begin therapy on his knee."

55

"I'm so glad you opted out of football and chose golf. He is going to be something that he called red-shirted this year. This is so he will still have all his eligibility when he gets better next year. He still gets four years of eligibility to play."

"Is he okay? Where is he?" asked Garney.

"He's in the family room with your father watching a Detroit Tigers baseball game. He's a bit down. Why don't you go see him? He was asking about how you were doing?"

"Sure, Mom, forget the cake. I'll have some later."

Maggie sighed and sat alone to eat the piece of cake as Garney left the kitchen with Wedge trailing just behind. She had to watch her weight if these conversations continued to end this way. Garney moved through the house to his father's favorite room. The 'family' room was expansive and filled with comfortable furniture. One of the focal points of the room was a massive stone fireplace. The other focal point in the family room was a large screen television set that was presently displaying a Detroit Tiger and Baltimore Orioles baseball game. Bo was resting comfortably with his injured leg elevated on an ottoman. Stephen Senior and Bo were in an animated conversation. They were discussing the prospects of the Detroit Lions football team for the approaching season.

Stephen's father was an ardent Detroit Lions fan, and they occasionally used Garney's grandparents' season tickets to go to a Lions home game. As his grandfather got older, the tickets became available more frequently. The Lions football team had moved to Ford Field in downtown Detroit from the Silverdome in Pontiac, Michigan. It made it a longer and more tedious trip to the Lion's home games. It was a much longer trip now that the Lions had relocated to downtown Detroit than when they played their home games in the stadium in Pontiac.

"Hey, Bo, what happened?"

"Blew my knee out, stupid thing; it wasn't even a hit. I just planted my foot to turn and cut in a practice drill, and it just gave away."

"How serious is it?

"Out for the season, but I probably wouldn't have played much this year anyway. The team depth chart had three or four running backs ahead of me. Two seniors and at least one junior."

"What about next year?" asked Garney.

Their father excused himself at that point, stating, "You boys have some catching up to do; the Tigers are losing, and I have some inventory paperwork that I should get done." They spoke in unison, "Okay, Dad," as their father left the room.

"The team physicians say it's just a badly strained or stretched ligament, and it's pretty clean. With a good rehab, I should be as good as new. I'll miss it, though, the practices, the trips, particularly the cheerleaders, and feeling part of the team. This is the first time I won't be playing football in September in six years. The coaches say I can be red-shirted so that I won't lose any of my four years of eligibility."

"I'm really sorry, Bo," Garney responded.

"What's up with you, Garn? You seem different, and you have that glow. Have you been getting your oil changed? Have you been playing hide the salami, layin' some pipe?"

Bo had a locker room humor that irritated his two brothers. His crassness was only used in the absence of their parents and other adults. Like his two Foster brothers, Bo too was considered to be a young gentleman when in the company of adults.

Garney turned crimson red in embarrassment and anger. One thing about Bo, he may not have been much of an academic, but he had an uncanny ability to be able to read people and situations. It was as if he had an extra sense, an intuition, that enabled him to be aware of situations by reading people and their body language.

Garney said, "Don't be such a pig; nothing's going on with me in that way." He knew immediately that Bo wasn't buying his response, that Bo didn't believe him. He asked, "When do you have to go back to university?"

"Changing the subject, that's a definite sign. I have to go back Sunday night."

Following that exchange, Bo changed the channel with the remote control. "Ball game is no good, and a Frasier rerun is coming on. I still don't believe you; I think you're hiding something. You've been getting it, haven't you?"

"Well, you're wrong, turkey; I've got nothing to hide. I have to get up early; I think I'll head to bed. Good to see you, Bo; sorry about your knee."

"Good night, Garn. See you tomorrow."

That night, Garney slept fitfully. He was on the early shift at the club the following day and struggled to get a whole night's rest. Wedge spent the night moving from position to position as his master rolled from one side of the bed to the other. Garney's had a last thought before he finally fell to sleep. If Bo suspected, would anyone else imagine? Had Bo heard something?

# Chapter 19: A Return to Normal

That autumn, Garney entered his senior year at high school and continued to work early mornings and Sundays at the country club. Some evenings and Saturdays were his time to play and practice his golf game as the season wound down. The high school football coach renewed his efforts to recruit Garney, now a senior, to join his football team. Garney was doubly sure after seeing Bo's injury that he wasn't remotely interested. To appease Mr. Birk, who coached other sports, he offered to attend track practices in the spring. Everyone knew the Foster boys were very fast sprinters on the track. State competition wide fast.

Occasionally, Garney saw Mr. And Mrs. Brophy at the country club and was pleased to see they had patched up their problems and seemed happy. He always remembered to refer to her as Mrs. Brophy, and she always insisted that he call her Carley. As the weeks passed, Garney felt certain that their secret was safe. He worried less and less frequently about their past indiscretions.

# Chapter 20: The Invite

Late that October, the golf season at the club was winding down. Soon, only the dining room would remain open during the weekends over the winter months from November to April. George Trent was in the process of closing the pro shop and was now readying for his migration south with the sun. George presently spent the winter in 'The Villages,' a golf paradise in central Florida between Ocala and Leesburg. As the daylight hours became shorter, George was eager to begin his annual trip to the warmer southern climate. Ben Atkinson remained at the golf course during the off-season. Along with a skeleton staff, they first closed the golf course, and then he repaired and winterized all the maintenance equipment and golf carts for the following season. George knew Ben was worth his weight in gold. Birch Run's equipment lasted far past its generally expected due date for replacement. Most other golf courses had a much shorter shelf life for their equipment.

On the last day, before the golf course was officially closed for the year, a light snowfall was changing the facility from an emerald green to an ivory white. The few cars that were standing in the member's parking lot were beginning to be covered with a fine coat of fresh white powder. Not even the most dedicated and avid golfers would attempt to get one more round in on a day like this. Understandably, no one was on the course. The car owners had come to pick up their golf clubs and clean out their lockers. Two card

61

games, likely gin rummy, were being played in the men's locker room. A fine haze of cigarette smoke was in the air as Garney entered the room seeking Mr. Trent. Much to the chagrin of most of the members, this was still the only part of the facility where smoking was permitted, and it was surely to be voted out at the next general meeting. Like in the rest of society, very few members of the club were still considered smokers. The majority of the other members wanted a smoke-free environment.

Garney had come to say his goodbyes for the winter to Mister Trent, his mentor, and Ben, the head greens-keeper. His father had mentioned to him in the morning that George had wanted to see him. Mr. Trent was seated at one of the tables involved in one of the card games, and he waved for Garney to come over to his table.

As the young man moved across the room, George spoke to one of the men standing, watching the card game unfold. "Bill, sit in and play for me for a few minutes. I want to talk to Garney."

Bill, who was a long-time club member and a high-handicap golfer, replied, "Sure, George, I can't do any worse than you're doing."

Another player at the table responded, "You better not be long, George. If Bill plays rummy like he plays golf, you won't be able to afford to go south this year." The group was still chuckling as Bill replaced George at the table, and Garney and George left for Mr. Trent's office. As they entered the office, George motioned to

Garney to take a seat as he moved around his desk to an oversized, comfortable-looking leather chair. The office was cluttered with paperwork, various golf clubs, and golf memorabilia. One shelf contained a considerable collection of wide-brimmed hats.

"Garney, I have been talking to your parents, and they have given me permission to discuss something with you." The way that Mr. Trent opened the conversation, Garney's immediate first thought was that someone knew his secret. He often felt pangs of guilt under the most ordinary circumstances. He blushed and tried to collect himself.

"What's that, Mr. Trent?"

"I am inviting you to come to my home in The Villages in Florida during your spring break to do a little golfing. I have never known such a dependable young employee, and I would like to repay you somehow. You take your time to think about it, and you can call or email me with your answer."

"I don't need any time, Mr. Trent. I would love to go to Florida to visit you and do some golfing. Thanks very much. It sounds terrific."

"There is one condition, Garney." "What's that, Mr. Trent?"

"Please stop calling me Mr. Trent. Please just call me George. You know, since I have known you, I have only seen you call one adult by their first name, and that was only a couple of times. You are an adult, and I want you to call me George."

"Who was that, Mr. Trent?"

George chuckled. "Carley Brophy, what does she have that I don't have?"

"I don't know, George," Garney smiled. He wished that he had not initially responded to the question. But he did recognize that he could use George's name for the first time.

They both laughed a little embarrassingly, and George stated, "I'd better get back to the card game while I still have a home in Florida. If Bill plays gin like the way he plays golf, the deal may be off. You call me in the Villages; your parents have my cell number there, and we'll work out the dates and details later. Ben is coming down in March, so maybe you can drive with him, or you could fly down and take the Village shuttle bus from the air terminal in Orlando. Thanks for all your good work, Garney; I'll see you in Florida sometime during the winter."

George reached into a desk drawer and removed a package and he handed it to Garney and said, "Here's a little something for you; go ahead and open it."

The young man removed the wrapping to discover an autographed copy of "The Feeling of Greatness," the story of Canadian golf legend Moe Norman.

# Chapter 21: Winter In Grayling

Garney felt an emptiness when the country club closed at the end of October. He concentrated on his studies for his scholarship and his father's grade point average demand. He daydreamed about the past summer events and his upcoming spring graduation. He recalled attending Steven and Bo's high school graduations and envied that they had finished high school and were already attending college. He didn't want to wish his life away, but Garney could hardly contain the excitement about his upcoming visit to Western Michigan University in Kalamazoo. He had settled on the dates for the golf trip to Florida and was looking forward to registering and attending the university next fall. Mr. Patterson had made it official; a full scholarship rather than a partial scholarship was his for the accepting. In February, Garney would sign a letter of intent for official acceptance into Western Michigan University. The scholarship was the first of the three scholarship offers that he received.

Starting in November of that year, Garney worked in the family business after school and on most Saturdays leading up to the Christmas season. Times were prosperous, and subsequently, it was a good season for the hardware store. They were doing a banner business. Hardware stores were no longer just tools and nuts and bolts. In many communities, these stores served as small department stores as well as suppliers for construction firms and the farmers' needs in the area. On one occasion, he had even assisted Carley Brophy in making a few purchases. Both of them couldn't help feeling awkward during the sales, but they never once mentioned or alluded to the previous summer. Garney still had deep feelings toward Carley, and even Carley could feel her attraction toward Garney, but the feelings were left unspoken. As she left the store, he couldn't help but notice her stunning figure, even though it was covered by her winter clothing.

Christmas was a wonderful holiday at the Foster household that season. Relatives migrated north to Grayling from the more southern parts of the state. This particular year, it was the northern part of the family's turn to host the other Hausens and the other Fosters. Over ten days, Maggie's parents, brothers and sisters, and Stephen's parents, brother and sister, and their families all visited for varying lengths of time. Steve and Bo were home from university. Everyone marveled at how Maggie could juggle the schedule of arrivals and departures and maintain such calmness. Maggie thrived on and loved every single minute of the holiday season. Her family and all her relatives were extremely important to her. She only wished that they could all live closer together.

During the fall semester, Bo had been dedicated to his rehabilitation program and was making a sound, steady recovery from his injury. His studies remained a concern to Maggie and Stephen as his grades did not seem to be a priority for Bo. He had assured his parents that he was doing fine. Maggie, in particular, wished he was as concerned about his classes as he was about his knee's medial ligament. The rest of the family seemed unaware that Bo's aim in life was to someday operate the family hardware business. University was just an avenue to prolong his participation in sports. In actuality, Bo was a homeboy and loved living in Grayling Michigan.

During the fall term at Bowling Green University, Garney's oldest brother Steve had met a co-ed, Jenny Marie, from Meadville, Pennsylvania. Arrangements had been made for Steve to spend some time with Jenny, visiting with her family on the last few days of the Christmas holiday. The eldest Foster son would be in Meadville in time for the New Year's Eve celebration. Steve was not enjoying the rigorous demands of the university hockey program. During the holiday, he had alluded to his parents that he might not play the following year, but he would complete this season.

The eldest Foster son had received permission from his Bowling Green coach to miss the annual Great Lakes Invitational Hockey Tournament in Detroit that Christmas. Missing a tournament was most unusual for Steve Junior. Steve still enjoyed the game, but the commitment to practice and constant travel were taking a toll on his academics. The hockey program was very proactive in assisting the players with their academics. His parents indicated that they would support their son in his decision. Not playing would result in losing his scholarship, but the financial repercussions were not as crucial as his long-range goals. Steve also revealed that he would like to finish his undergraduate degree at Bowling Green University. His parents assumed that the young lady from Pennsylvania would likely have influenced his decision.

Garney's gift that Christmas from his parents was a new golf bag. He spent Christmas afternoon cleaning his golf clubs and loading the bag with all of his necessary golf paraphernalia. Even though it was still a couple of months away, he was preparing for his trip to the Villages in Florida. Garney would not accept any money from his parents for his visit to Mr. Trent's winter home and was adamant that he would pay for everything from his savings. Garney phoned his mentor George the next day to notify him of the dates of his arrival and departure and also to wish him a happy holiday.

# Chapter 22: Kalamazoo

Following the new year, the winter in Michigan became particularly severe. The short days and long nights seemed to have no end. For Garney, each week seemed to go on indefinitely. The school system had more closings due to the winter storms than any school term in recent memory. School bus cancellations were far more common than they had ever been during any of the Foster boys' elementary or secondary school educations. It had been a rare occurrence for the school buses not to run. The radio stations in the community were constantly tuned in for the early morning school bus and local road reports. Students and teachers alike initially enjoyed the reprieves from the school routine, but even they grew weary of the disruptions. Parents, school board members, and administrators grew more concerned as the winter wore on. There were rumors that the school spring break might have to be canceled.

Garney enjoyed the days off at the beginning of the storms, but before long, he managed to fight through the less severe winter conditions to drive to his high school. He would arrive at the school in the family 4x4 to collect his schoolwork. Garney had grown concerned about his grades, his SATs, and his academic acceptance into Western Michigan University.

The young man dreamed of his impending golfing holiday in Florida with George, his return to the golf and country club in the spring, and his eventual registration at the university in Kalamazoo.

He was more certain than ever that he preferred the color green to the color white.

Garney had scheduled a campus trip in February to Kalamazoo. The trip was a campus visitation to officially accept his golf scholarship. He was eager to see the campus and the facilities that would be his home away from home for the next four years.

Maggie and Stephen had arranged to accompany him on that visitation weekend. They would first make a stopover in Frankenmuth to visit with Maggie's parents and then only Stephen would travel with Garney across the state to Kalamazoo.

Garney was surprised at the size of the city, which was about one hundred thousand in population. The odd name Kalamazoo had its origins with the native peoples of the continent. The Native American word meant "place where the water boils."

The meeting and the campus tour with Dave Patterson and one of the senior members of the golf team were enjoyable, lasting about two hours. After the tour, the Foster father and son spent part of the afternoon meandering around the campus. Garney expressed reservations to his father about leaving a community where it was possible to know almost everyone by name to live in a city where most people would be strangers to each other.

It was a bitter February day, and the weather didn't enhance Garney's first impression of the city with the catchy name. Stephen assured his son that it would be a culture shock for anyone from a small community to leave their home for a much larger community. He assured Garney that the vast majority of young people thrived on their change to a campus lifestyle. He was making the proper decision. He had to move on to the next stage in his life. Kalamazoo would have an entirely different aura in the fall when he started his full-time attendance at the university. As usual, his father was right. The following autumn was the most splendid fall the state had seen in two decades, and Kalamazoo was no exception. The colors were stunning.

# Chapter 23: Winter Storms

As winter wore on, the days began to lengthen, and gray was still the predominant color. Garney had talked to Ben a few times and had even taken a drive to the country club just to look at the golf course. On one occasion, he had gone out of his way to drive past the Brophy home, just for old times' sake, he rationalized.

In late February, there had been a trip to East Lansing, Michigan, to attend a Bowling Green-Michigan State hockey game. The Fosters watched most of Steven's games on a streaming university network service. This was the only game close enough for the family to attend in person. Steve played with great energy, and even though the Orange and Brown Falcons lost the game to the Green and White Spartans, he was the most dangerous player on his team. Playing in front of his family seemed to bring out the best in the eldest Foster son. He hadn't been having a particularly good season playing hockey for the Falcons that year. Maggie, who had watched her sons participate in sports since childhood, covered her eyes several times due to the game's physical nature. She secretly hoped that her son would relinquish his scholarship after this season. Even Bo had been able to attend the game with two of his friends from Ann Arbor and the University of Michigan campus. A brief but happy reunion with Steve before the Falcon team bus departed made the two-and-a-half-hour trip from Grayling seem worthwhile. As a junior, Steve enjoyed a berth on the bus, which made the return trip to the Ohio campus more bearable. There were several sleeping berths on the team's travel bus, which were allotted in order of seniority to the team members. Seniors first, juniors second, sophomores third, and freshmen low man on the totem pole.

March came in like a lion! There was a local school board concern about the lost time from classes at the high school. The inclement weather increased the possibility of canceling the school's spring break, which was now only three weeks away. Garney prayed for a reprieve from the winter storms. His trip to the Villages was in jeopardy. Finally, a decision was made by the school board administrators. The spring break could be held on schedule if there were no further disruptions to the classes and the student's education. Winter sports schedules had been canceled, and the basketball teams, in particular, were affected. Scholarship offers were in jeopardy. The school musical was postponed, affecting an entirely different section of the student body. Weather played havoc on more than the academics in the school. Garney became an amateur meteorologist over the next two weeks. He watched the Weather Channel and the local forecasts before retiring to his room each evening. Cold fronts from neighboring Canada stayed north of Michigan's northern peninsula. The midwestern low fronts and their accompanying storms blew through Chicago and shuffled off to Buffalo, staying south of the Great Lakes. Most of Michigan was spared any more of winter's wrath.

As the days approached for Garney's visit with George, he began to include Florida in his weather watch. He was delighted with what he observed. Florida's climate was holding true to form. The climate above and below the imaginary line that ran from Tampa on the west coast to Daytona Beach on the east coast was seasonably glorious. The town of Frostproof straddled that imaginary line and was situated just south of the Villages.

When the day approached for Garney's scheduled departure, the travel plans were made for Maggie to drive him to the Detroit air terminal. Maggie's trip south to Detroit included her plans to visit her parents in her hometown of Frankenmuth. She would visit with her family for two days upon returning from the Metropolitan Airport. Garney had his clothes and golf equipment packed and ready to go well in advance of his scheduled flight south. Garney did not have much persuading to do when he suggested they leave after Friday's classes and stay overnight at his grandparents on the way to the air terminal. His flight to Orlando was scheduled for late Saturday afternoon. The young man knew that Frankenmuth was much closer to his departure point, and in the event of a sudden storm, he stood a much better chance of not missing his flight. No storm was in the forecast. A storm of another type would become a more significant concern.

# Chapter 24: The Fight

It was a Friday in mid-March during the last day of classes leading into the spring reading break. Garney was in attendance at school but only physically. His mind wandered, and he constantly daydreamed during the morning classes. All he could visualize were palm trees and green golf courses.

A special career assembly for graduating students was scheduled in the auditorium during the afternoon. Several guest speakers were to make career presentations to the senior class. Garney had asked his parents if he could be excused from the assembly that afternoon as he had already chosen his career. He rationalized that his early dismissal from school would allow him and his mother to have daylight driving hours on their trip to the Hausen household in Frankenmuth. Maggie and Stephen liked the idea but did not bite nor agree to his suggestion. He was to remain in school for the balance of that scheduled school day.

The school auditorium served a multitude of purposes, and it had recently been remodeled and renovated. The theatre provided a site for assemblies, graduations, school theatre productions, musical concerts, and special community functions. Its appearance and style were not unlike many other secondary school community facilities throughout the country. Rich red curtains with gold fringe and tassels, gold-painted columns, and newly installed red velour seats made it the pride of the school and the community. The three aisles, one center and two at the sides, sloped from the back entrances to the raised stage at the front.

The school staff members directed the senior students to the rows located in the front third of the auditorium. It seemed perhaps the date and time for the career presentation was ill-chosen. Although the students were soon to graduate, their thoughts were more on the impending holiday than their futures.

More than a few students were redirected by the staff, who were monitoring the school exit doors, to go to the auditorium for the assembly. Some seniors were attempting to begin their vacation a little earlier. A few more were escorted and directed from the washrooms as they attempted to wait out the start of the gathering for an early departure from the school. Not surprisingly, the senior students were unusually restless as they moved down the aisles to their seats near the front of the theatre. To Garney's utter surprise and dismay, just as the students were settling down, Carley Brophy entered the auditorium stage with several other guest speakers.

Carley was representing the local real estate board. She was dressed very professionally, and she was stunning. An audible murmur swept through the room as she walked across the stage to take her seat along with the others. A few catcalls and whistles from his peers caused Garney to rage inwardly. A comment from directly behind him, "Look at the fucking hooters on that," was the last straw. He turned around and directed the oaf to shut his big mouth. Now that the other student was challenged in front of his peers, he had to react. The offender pushed Garney violently in the back of the head. Garney didn't recall what happened next, but he snapped for the first time in his life. He climbed over his seat and beat the other male student savagely. It took several other students and some staff members to pull him off his victim.

Garney's next recollection was talking to a Michigan State Trooper in a vice principal's office. His actions meant he was possibly going to be charged with assault. A young female student, the victim's girlfriend, had received a mouse above her eye, and a supposed dislocated shoulder sat on a bench in the waiting area outside the school office. The young male was on his way to the hospital with a split lip, loosened teeth, and a possible concussion. Garney's parents had been summoned and were en route to the local secondary school.

There were two things in the young Foster's favor, but still, his situation seemed bleak. His family's reputation and his record were highly recommended by the school administrator who was present in the office. The other combatant had been in and out of trouble with the community and the school system since his primary years and was well known to the local police. He should have graduated two years before this date but remained behind due to his poor academic record. There was suspicion that if you wanted any illegal drugs, he was the best source to obtain the contraband. The State Trooper was seeking answers as to what had precipitated the altercation. Garney feared to explain his reaction because of his past relationship with Carley Brophy.

Stephen and Maggie arrived at the school, eased the Foster hardware truck into a visitor's parking space, and quickly found their way to the administrative offices. As they approached the front desk, a young receptionist rose from her chair to greet them.

"Hello, Mister and Missus Foster. If you will follow me, I'll show you to Mister Quinn's office." Garney's parents nodded, and they were led toward a large office located to the left of the reception area. As they moved across the room, both of them felt the gaze on their backs by others in the area.

Even though both of the Fosters had been in this building on more positive occasions, they now felt considerable discomfort in being in this publicly owned and operated facility. Their discomfort was heightened on this occasion and in this unusual situation, and they felt like intruders. Other parents who had been here before them, in similar situations caused by the negative behavior of their offspring, could attest to their feeling of despair.

# Chapter 25: Steve And Maggie Go to School

Principal Ross Quinn met them at his office door, ushered them into his room, and offered them chairs as he moved behind his desk to an oversized leather swivel chair. The carpeted room was moderately spacious and contained a few green plants. Pictures of two state football championship teams hung on one wall, education diplomas on another wall. A filing cabinet completed the decor. The desk was void of anything except obligatory pictures of his family, a pen in a holder, and a leather-bound blotter. The principal was quite distinguished. Dressed in a dark brown pin-striped suit, white on a white dress shirt, brightly painted tie, and a full head of silver hair. He was the picture of authority. Ross Quinn was well respected and admired by the community, as well as the staff and students at the school. The school administrator asked them to please be seated. They both sat in the visitors' chairs facing his desk. Mister Quinn apprised them of the situation and indicated that Garney was not offering any explanation or reason for his attack on the other student. Mr. Quinn also stated that he had spoken to four student witnesses, and three had indicated that Garney had not initiated the altercation.

They all declared that the other student had, quote, "sucker punched Garney in the head from behind." A young female, the victim's girlfriend, was adamant Garney had "started the fuckin fight." The other combatant was probably going to be okay, with no permanent damage, just damage to his pride and reputation. His dignity was less intact than his physical well-being, but he knew the legal system and indicated he might press charges. Other staff members stated that student witnesses, friends of the injured student, suggested that the attack was unprovoked. Something that both the school and police officials questioned. The school's position would probably be a suspension of some duration after the school spring holiday. The school and the board of education had a zero-violence policy. Maggie asked anxiously, "When can we see Garnet?"

The principal replied, "We can go to the vice-principal's office now. Maybe one of you can get an explanation from Garney as to what precipitated the altercation."

The three of them moved solemnly through the office area. They passed by the young girl and two of her friends, who were seated on a bench in the reception section of the area.

Stephen noticed the small bandage above her eye. The multiple earrings in her nose, tongue, ears, and eyebrows completed a rather bizarre picture. The dislocation of her shoulder had been exaggerated as it was in full swing in their direction. She was still able to give them a huge swinging one-finger salute after they passed. The bump did not require any further medical attention. She was waiting to be interviewed by the trooper as a witness.

Ross Quinn rapped gently on the vice-principal's door. His announcement of their arrival was made only out of courtesy as the state trooper and the vice-principal had gestured for them to enter as they approached. Garney rose to his feet when his parents and the Principal entered the room, and he politely offered his chair to his mother. Maggie was very near tears as she accepted her young son's offer.

Without waiting for introductions, Maggie looked up to her youngest son and asked, "Garnet, why were you in a fight?"

Garney offered an explanation for the first time and quickly replied, "I didn't start it, Mom. He said something, I said something, he pushed me from behind, and I just lost it. I'm sorry it happened."

His father was shaking hands with the vice-principal, whom he recognized but did not know personally, and the state trooper Harvey Guidry, who was a friend and teammate on his Wednesday night Antiques hockey team. On hearing Garney's response, Stephen turned quickly and asked, "You say you didn't start the fight?"

Garney stared at the floor for an extended period. He was confused. He had become good at deceiving his parents this past August. He knew his father's hockey mentality condoned sudden retaliatory fights but knew what he had done in this situation was probably wrong. He stared at the gray and white landscape outside the office window and finally responded as honestly as he dared.

"In a way, we're both responsible, but I guess I started the actual fight."

Harvey Guidry interrupted his friend's son and asked, "Why didn't you say something earlier, Garney?"

Garney just shrugged and returned his gaze out of the office window. He realized that for the first time, his trip to Florida was in jeopardy, and a sick feeling washed through his entire frame.

Trooper Guidry, turning towards Stephen, said, "Swamp, you and Mrs. Foster can take Garney home now; no charges have been laid, but depending on the Turcotte lad, Garney's not out of the woods yet. After I question the little lady out there, I will be going to the hospital to question Shawn. I'll be in touch with you later today or tomorrow. I think it's best that Garney stays home until you hear from me or someone in the department."

The small group began to leave the office and move through the administrative area after saying perfunctory thank you and goodbyes. The vice principal and the trooper turned and returned to the office from which they had just departed.

As the Fosters made their way to the main exit from the offices, the young girl leaped to her feet and screamed at Garney, "You fuckin asshole, I hope you go to jail, you asshole, you're a dead man."

Maggie and Garney stopped in their tracks. Stephen gently placed his hands on their backs and ushered them forward and out the door. "Enough drama for one day," Stephen murmured. Stephen turned to Maggie and said jokingly, "Isn't she sweet? Aren't you glad we had sons?"

At the same time, the administrators and the trooper were directing a somewhat hysterical young female toward the vice principal's office.

The ride home from the high school was driven in silence. Garney's thoughts leaped from Carley – to his trip to Florida – to the possible charges he faced – to his parents' disappointment – to Shawn Turcotte – to a potential loss of his scholarship. He must keep Carley Brophy's name out of the situation. Would his trip be canceled? Would he have a criminal record? Would his parents forgive him? Was Shawn all right? Would this affect his scholarship? Garney's head ached, and he felt nauseous. Why hadn't his parents allowed him to miss the afternoon assembly and leave for Frankenmuth early? He felt this would all have been avoided.

As they entered the house, Wedge was at the door. Like other faithful pets, the cat had unconditional love no matter what his master had done. Garney scooped Wedge up in his arms and stroked its back. The tortoise-shelled pet purred loudly, seeming to sense something was amiss. Wedge was particularly affectionate that afternoon as if the pet knew Garney was deeply bothered by something.

As he removed his coat, Stephen turned to Garney and said, "Go to the family room. We'll be right there. I want to talk to your mother."

What seemed like an eternity, ten minutes later, Maggie and Stephen entered the family room and took a place on the sofa facing Garney. Maggie sighed, and his father cleared his throat. Garney interpreted this as a very ominous sign.

Stephen began, "Your mother and I have decided that if the police department gives its approval, you may visit George in Florida. We do realize that this incident is completely out of character for you. It is going to depend on when the police contact us. Time is running out as you have a flight tomorrow that you are scheduled to catch. It also will depend on whether it is legal to leave the state if there are any charges laid against you. We both feel you are being evasive and not giving us the complete story. Our approval depends on your more complete explanation."

Garney started to speak, and his father raised his hand, gesturing Garney to remain silent until he was finished speaking. Stephen began again, "Even if the police phone today, leaving for your grandparents' tonight is out of the question. Your mother is far too upset to drive."

The phone rang as Stephen began to speak again. His father stopped just as he began. Maggie said, "Can you get it, Stephen? I can't talk right now."

The call was from Trooper Guidry, and the conversation lasted about five minutes. Stephen listened, and his part of the conversation consisted of nods and uh-huh. Only at the termination

84

of the conversation did Stephen offer any additional words. "Thanks for what you have done, Harv. I feel better knowing the situation and that the other lad is fine. Thanks again, Harv."

For Maggie and Garney, Stephen's dearth of conversation seemed to make time stand still. Only his closing remarks brought any relief to their anxious and very tense waiting.

After ten minutes of conversation, the situation became somewhat more straightforward. Garney revealed his anger at the treatment of the guest speakers and the sequence of events that led to the altercation. He hadn't lied, but he hadn't been entirely truthful. Stephen explained that the other student had required a few stitches and received a large bump on the back of his head. Shawn Turcotte had said that he didn't need the assistance of the cops; he could take care of himself, and he would handle it. Even Shawn knew better than to risk another fight with Garney, as he would be completely outmatched again. He needed to sound good to his peers. He even dreaded the possibility of any reoccurrence of the drubbing he had received.

Before he retired that evening, Garney checked the weather forecasts, and he was relieved to see clear and cold in Michigan was the predominant theme. The family went to bed early that night as Garney and Maggie intended to leave at daybreak for Frankenmuth and then the Metropolitan Airport which was located just outside of Detroit. As he left the family room, Garney kissed his mother on the forehead and thanked his parents for their support and their understanding. He apologized for losing his control and letting them down. Wedge followed Garney to his room, and both the young man and his pet slept fitfully again that night.

As they fell asleep, Maggie and Stephen both reflected on the day's events. Neither would admit it to the other, but they were both proud of their youngest son. Their pride was for different reasons. His mother admired his standing up against what was wrongful behavior toward the guest speakers, even though his reaction was unpopular among some of his peers. His father was proud of his combative abilities, which were popular among some of his peers. Garney could more than take care of himself.

# Chapter 26: Trip On

Stephen had topped up the family vehicle with gas and checked the essential fluid levels the previous evening. Maggie would use the family suburban, which had 4x4 traction control. Even though the following few days' weather report did not predict any snowfall, one had to consider the possibility of the drifting of existing snow along the highway. He considerately remembered to place a spare bottle of windshield washer fluid in the rear compartment for safety reasons. Garney's father wanted to ensure a safe and secure journey for his loved ones. He would worry until he was assured that his wife Maggie had delivered their son to the Detroit air terminal and was safely at her parent's home. Only an obligatory phone call home indicating a safe arrival would allow him to relax. Stephen would delay departing for the store that day until his family was safely on their way south. He had charged her cellular phone overnight to ensure that it was ready if it were to be required. As they were departing, his last warning was, "Be sure you use the four-wheel drive both ways."

The mother and son departed from Grayling just before daybreak. The white Blazer moved south on Interstate seventy-five with Maggie at the wheel. The arrangement was for the two to share the driving en route to Detroit. Interstate seventy-five was a main artery that wound its way north and south from northern Michigan to southern Florida. It passed various types of geography from the plains of Ohio, the rolling hills of Kentucky and Tennessee, to increasing warmth through the stately pines of Georgia to the final destination, the beaches of Florida. It was a favorite route for both truckers and, during the winter months in the fall and the spring, the snowbirds. Garney was pleased he was only driving a portion of Interstate seventy-five in Michigan. His flight south would place him in Orlando about two days sooner than those driving to a similar vacation destination.

# Chapter 27: The Airport

Everything was the color of gray as the landscape this time of year seemed reluctant to release its grasp on the winter season.

Other than being buffeted by a raw, westerly wind, the Blazer traveled smoothly over the bare interstate expressway. Garney and his mother drove in silence as the rural landscape passed by them. Farmlands, the exits, highway signs, and billboards seemed a continuous blur. The traffic was initially very light. Only two cars and a brewery transport truck had passed heading north on the other side of the median. Mile after mile, the Fosters followed one set of taillights some distance ahead of them, and the headlights of another vehicle followed them at about a distance of half a mile.

Maggie could wait no longer. "Garnet, there is some fruit in that bag on the back seat. Would you like an apple or an orange?"

Garney sat upright and wondered what was coming as he replied, "No thanks, but can I get you something?"

"Garnet, was your altercation about a girl?"

The young man stammered, "No, what makes you think that?"

"It's just a mother's instinct and your evasiveness, that's all. You do believe in female intuition, don't you?"

"No, Mom, you're the only lady in my life right now." Garney's mind was trying to quickly come up with another topic so that he could change this conversation. "Do you want me to take over the driving now?"

"Okay, just wondering. We had a feeling that you were seeing someone who we weren't aware of last summer. That seemed unlike you not to tell us, and I guess we were wrong."

The young man's face reddened without replying, but inwardly, all he could think of was, where is the airport? When will we get there? How much longer? Finally, after a pause in the conversation, a large highway sign came into sight, indicating the airport exit was three miles ahead. Almost there. Fifteen minutes later, he was unloading his golf clubs and luggage from the rear of the 4X4. He kissed his mother on the cheek and told her to drive safely and be careful as she was heading to Frankenmuth for a visit with her family.

# Chapter 28: The Flight

Garney passed through security, checked his baggage and his golf clubs, and headed for his departure gate. Much to his relief, they arrived at Detroit Metropolitan Airport early, and the flight departure was on time. Garney was beginning to temporarily leave his problems behind. When he checked in and had his seat assigned, the young man silently prayed that his golf clubs would arrive on the same flight that he was boarding for Orlando. He was aware that stranger things had happened. After the flight's first call, he was soon boarding the airplane and locating his seat.

About twenty minutes later, the Southwest 727 airline growled into the sky. As it entered the clouds above, the passenger jet started to miniaturize the buildings, runways, homes, and vehicles below.

The obligatory safety video with an attractive flight attendant waving her arms and pointing her hands in unison was followed by the seatbelt and no smoking regulations. Garney was fascinated by her hands and wondered if other passengers dismissed the instructions as quickly as he had.

In the event of a serious problem, he was sure that very few others on the plane had the slightest idea of where to go or what to do. Garney did recall something about following some red and white lights on the floor. He felt assured that they would have a quick review amidst the chaos if it became necessary and urgent. He

91

promised himself that he would be more attentive should this occur. In the meantime, he had to trust that there were enough conscientious first-time passengers and nervous fliers who were well-versed in the safety procedures.

Garney was seated next to the window, which at this point only offered a view of the blanket of clouds beneath them. He had noted, before the departure, while waiting in his seat, a middle-aged passenger in the row ahead of him was reading author Erica Jong's "Fear of Flying." The young man pondered, "Why would you read that on a flight?" Reading and literature were not one of Garney's strong points. He only wanted to let his mind wander and imagine. This he was quite capable of doing.

By the luck of the draw, he was seated next to a lingerie sales representative from Hamtramck, Michigan, a Polish community located within the environs of Detroit. The man's youngish teenage son occupied the third seat. The salesman, much to the young son's chagrin and discomfort, orated his life history along with his son's competitive swimming feats and successes. Garney did not have the slightest interest in either subject. He wondered about people who gave total strangers details of their lives, which they didn't disclose to people who were very close to them. Even the airline food had a redeeming quality as his seatmate ceased his discussion of women's undergarments. Garney now knew which were demographically the largest and smallest breasted states. He did recall that Michigan was rated in the top ten, and Garney surmised that Carley Brophy was undoubtedly doing her share. The salesman's son also seemed to be less uncomfortable as the bra and panty representative was silent when his mouth contained a portion of his meal. The son on one side and Garney on the other continually offered their small salads, rolls, and desserts to the father, keeping him occupied and, for the most part, silent. As he leaned forward to place his apple cobbler on his father's tray, America's next, Michael Phelps, winked at Garney. They both were aware of the game and the glorious silence it produced. Mister Maidenform was a large individual and was very appreciative of the two boys' offerings. The more food, the better.

Orlando International Airport was a relatively easy terminal to navigate. Soon after touchdown and a train shuttle to the main airport, Garney and George were shaking hands in greetings. George had opted to meet Garney at the airport rather than have him use the Village's shuttle service. The previous twenty-four hours were temporarily washed from his memory and his system. A couple of toll roads and an expressway later, they had arrived in the Villages.

While collecting his luggage and golf clubs from the carousel, the young man answered his mentor's questions about the flight, the weather, and the happenings in Michigan. Nothing was asked about his recent altercation, and nothing was offered.

Florida's warmth seemed to envelop his entire being as they exited the terminal through the automatic doors. He was now certain he knew why Mr. Trent and others migrated to the south when the winter season showed signs of arriving at higher latitudes. Not only did he want to become a golf professional, but he also wanted to settle in the southern states for the winter season every year.

When they arrived in the Villages community, Garnet was astonished at the wonder of this property. There were golf courses and more golf courses. There were facilities and more facilities. Golf carts of all colors, shapes, and sorts were being used as a second family vehicle, traveling here and there to golf courses and town centers, of which there were a number. The town squares, each with a different theme, were active with residents and visitors alike.

George lived in a courtyard villa, which was tastefully decorated, and in a community of about 80 other villas, with each one landscaped neatly. His villa overlooked an executive course, of which there were many. All the championship courses had country club facilities, a pro shop, a restaurant, a pool, tennis courts, and other amenities. Most of the residents were 55 years of age and over, and probably one of the most active communities in the nation. There were two thirty-two-lane bowling facilities and a daily newspaper that kept people up to date on the activities that were being offered daily and weekly. Pool halls, pickleball courts, and all other imaginable facilities. Something for everyone.

A wonderful week followed. Golf was followed by more golf. On two separate days, George left Garney at the course, and he played an additional eighteen holes with a few of George's resident friends. George had his favorite golf course among the many village courses but had booked other championship courses for Garney to have a complete golfing experience.

Mr. Trent played his best golf during the winter months, free from all of the responsibilities associated with operating Birch Run Country Club.

Wonderful meals, restaurants, and lounging around one of the many local pools completed some of the days. A trip to a theme park in Orlando was canceled to accommodate more golf during the week. One afternoon, George arranged an appointment for Garney with one of the teaching professionals at a golf lesson facility on the Village's property. Early evenings were occasionally spent at one of the downtown squares, enjoying the live entertainment offered at each of the downtown gazebos. One thing Garney found frustrating was the obligatory use of electric golf carts on the courses. Garney would have much preferred to have walked and carried his clubs, but the country club rules prevented him from doing so. Not once did he watch the Weather Channel as each beautiful day was followed by another. The temperature each day was the same as yesterday, the same as tomorrow would be.

The vacation ended too soon, and before long, he was on his flight north. Not long after, he was traveling north on Interstate seventy-five with his mother and father, who had met him at the airport in Detroit. Even Wedge had made the trip to greet his master.

Stephen had insisted on accompanying Maggie to Detroit because of a possible impending late March winter storm. Wedge's inclusion in the trip south was strictly Maggie's idea.

# Chapter 29: The Summer

Spring arrived, and the golf season appeared anew with all of its usual devotees and a plethora of new disciples. Golf continued to become one of the fastest-growing recreational activities in North America. The snowbirds began to migrate north, and those that had remained in Michigan emerged from their hibernation. They were about to resume and start their quest to subdue an activity that refused to be subdued. Golf! The neophytes did not know what fate awaited them. Some would leave the game in frustration; others would struggle to succeed in a game that, to some, resembled an opiate. They would never win.

Problems disappeared for Garney that spring. The troubled Sean Turcotte had not filed charges. A brief glaring down in a school hallway put the feud to rest. Although goaded by his peers, the repeat juvenile offender knew that another confrontation with Garney would likely lead to the same result. Discretion was the better part of his valor. Sean's success with his peers was attributed to stealth, not face-to-face disputes. He was better suited for theft and vandalism or deviant behavior, which was not observable by others. Garney's penalty for his part in the assembly conflict was a three-day in-school suspension. He was excluded from classes and worked in a detention room. It seemed to be a strange place for the young Foster. He was sequestered in a small room across from the school offices with other students serving time for various offenses of negative behavior. He worked independently at assigned classroom work with the school's rogue gallery, who in turn were trying hard not to accomplish anything academic that might lead to their future success.

True to his word, Garney competed for the school track and field team that spring. He finished second in the district 100-yard dash and anchored the winning relay team to victory. Mr. Birk burst with pride as the school sent 12 athletes to the state track and field championships, which were held that year in Saginaw. A city that is geographically located on Michigan's thumb.

Summer passed somewhat uneventfully. Carley and Nick Brophy sold their home that summer. They moved to the Carolinas for a better climate and a new start. Some of their earlier problems had resurfaced, and once again, the Brophy couple were arguing regularly in private. Garney's past secret seemed safe forever. In a twist of irony, Garney's parents had looked at the Brophy home when it first appeared on the local real estate market. Maggie fell in love with how Carley had decorated the interior of her home. On the other hand, Stephen was adamant that he would not purchase a home with a swimming pool.

During dinner one evening, Maggie extolled the house's virtues. She declared to Garney, "I love Carley's taste; you should see what she has done to the master bedroom!"

Garney politely excused himself from the table on the pretense of an oncoming headache. He secretly prayed that his father

98

would not be swayed from his stance of not having a swimming pool. Garney was worrying needlessly. Stephen would never leave the home that contained so many happy memories for their family.

The summer season passed quickly, and the official start of fall was only three weeks away. Garney Foster became apprehensive and yet excited. Soon, he would have a change of address for most of his next four years. He was entering the next phase of his life and the independence and responsibility that would accompany the enormous step of leaving home.

# Chapter 30: Bo Returns Home

Four years passed too quickly. The Foster family in Grayling saw these years slip by routinely. Initially, Wedge pined for his young master, refusing to eat for a while every time Garney returned to his campus. Maggie would become concerned, but soon, the feline returned to its regular eating habits. Wedge grew accustomed to the sporadic visits from Garney and his return each summer for a more extended stay. Wedge was becoming more and more Maggie's cat.

There was only one significant disruption from routine during Garney's college years. Brother Bo's grades became abysmal, and he left the University of Michigan after the first semester of his sophomore year. Bo had not completely recovered from his knee injury. The young Wolverine had rehabilitated his knee with passion but to no avail. He was unable to return to his previous success and was limited to a few playing minutes during his sophomore year when the game was one-sided for one team or the other. He returned home after completing the football season and a seasonal football bowl game, which seemed to be a Michigan tradition. He neglected to inform his parents that he hadn't attempted to write most of his term examinations.

Bo became assistant manager of Foster's hardware store, which he had long believed to be his destiny. He enjoyed it and was very accomplished at it.

Bo became depressed at times as things were not as he remembered. He had failed to factor in that most of his friends were no longer hometown residents. Some were attending various educational institutions in and out of state, some had enlisted in the military, and a few more were working out of the area. Summers passed by more quickly when his college friends returned to Grayling. Bo seemed jealous of his peer's successes. The rest of the year, he seemed lonely. Swamp and Maggie became concerned about their middle son's apparent lack of purpose. He spent many of his days during the year working and, in the evening, watching television, which became too big a part of Bo's daily routine.

He was gaining too much weight. Like many sedentary ex-athletes, his diet hadn't changed much, but his activity pattern had been drastically reduced. Maggie became concerned as proper meals, even for a cat, were essential to her.

In Garney's final year in Kalamazoo, his brother Bo indicated to his parents that he was considering attending Eastern Michigan University in Ypsilanti to complete his education. Maggie, in particular, was hopeful and elated that he might decide to return to his education with a renewed purpose.

The eldest son in the family completed his degree at Bowling Green University. Steven was now attending law school at the University of Miami in Ohio, and he had become engaged to Jenny Marie from Meadville. Swamp and Maggie adored her, finally a surrogate daughter! In his final year as a senior, Steven remained in the Falcon hockey program and maintained his scholarship while at Bowling Green University. His hockey skills blossomed in his final year, and the New York Islanders of the National Hockey League drafted him in the fifth round of the NHL entry draft. Steven Junior knew that his abilities would, at best, lead to a journeyman role in a top minor professional league. Other than cursory contact with the NHL Islanders, he left the matter behind him. Hockey had provided him with a good education. He was flattered to have been drafted, but he knew a passion for the game was necessary to have a successful career in professional sports. He lacked the total commitment essential to successfully play the game professionally. Bo couldn't fathom this decision and was stunned that his older brother would pass up an opportunity to turn professional. Maggie was thrilled, and Swamp was a very proud father on draft day, as hockey was his first love. Swamp walked with a spring in his step for days after the draft of players to the NHL was announced. The area locals were equally proud that a native son had been chosen in the annual June NHL selection process. However, Swamp supported his eldest son when he announced that he had chosen law school over a possible hockey career. Swamp, in his old-timer hockey, played with several teammates who, when they were younger, almost made a career in the professional ranks. Now they couldn't leave not making the grade of turning professional behind them. Woulda, coulda, shoulda.

# Chapter 31: Western Michigan

During his four years at Western Michigan University, Garney achieved excellent grades and played solid golf. This was particularly true in his final intercollegiate golf season. In his last year, he was selected captain and most valuable player of the university golf team. As a senior, the youngest Foster son was selected to the third team of the NCAA All-American Collegiate Golf Team. His playing handicap was now a one.

Garney lived in a college residence during his freshman year in Kalamazoo. During his last three years, he shared nearby campus facilities with new friends. The young Foster and Paul Barkley, a Canadian student who also participated on the college golf team, shared living quarters with Eric Stayner and Arish Hamallid. Eric and Arish were fellow marketing students from the Detroit area who had grown up and attended high school together. Eric and Arish took it as their responsibility to travel to Kalamazoo each summer. There, they would arrange living accommodations for the quartet for the upcoming school year. These young men were serious about their studies, and all were met with appropriate success. They competed with friendly bets, usually pizza and beer, on their grades, common course test results, and grade point average. This, in a small way, contributed to their excellent results. It might be noted that Arish rarely, if ever, had to buy drinks or food.

During the four years at the Western Michigan Campus, they garnered good times and memories. During their undergraduate years, the four young men resided in three various houses in an older residential area that could have served as a setting for a Norman Rockwell painting. Older two and three-story brick homes with front and side verandahs, gingerbread trim, high ceilings, and large mature shade trees were the norm for the neighborhood. The young men rode their bicycles to and from classes in the spring and fall. In the winter, they walked or used the local transit system to commute to their classes and their studies. This was a life repeated by many other young women and men, year after year across the nation, in their quest for an education and a future in their chosen field of study.

Football Saturdays in the fall, late-night sessions working on assignment deadlines, preparing for examinations, keg parties and pep rallies, pizza diets, and fraternity or sorority parties came and went. Most students were able to juggle these events along with their studies and survive. Due to their social life, others were not as successful, and their faces soon disappeared from the campus setting. These students didn't lack the ability, for the most part, just the motivation and the perspective of why they were in attendance at the university. After being away for a semester or two, some of these students returned to college with a renewed purpose. Others would begin careers often in occupations their parents had not foreseen a few years ago. "Fries with your order." Occasionally, others would not complete their studies for financial reasons. Coach Patterson had always made his charges fully aware that the vast majority of college athletes would not earn a living on the field of play but rather from their academic pursuits.

Before his freshman year, Garney was upgraded from a partial to a full scholarship. The financial upgrade was not as significant to him as this recognition of his achievements. In the final semester of his graduating year, he faced a dilemma and a major decision. Knowing what he desired to do, the young man consulted his parents, golf coach Dave Patterson, and mentor George for advice and approval.

After attending a campus recruiting and careers exposition, Garney was offered a position with a major marketing firm in Omaha, Nebraska. What he had worked for academically was in his grasp. His initial reason for choosing marketing and similar business courses was to better manage the finances and the operation of a golf and country club. Garney rationalized that the state of Nebraska was too far from his Michigan roots. He felt sure his mother would support that decision. He felt confident that George or Coach Patterson, through their circle of golfing contacts, would be able to assist him in locating an assistant golf professional position with an accredited golf and country club in an area closer to his roots.

Much to his surprise, Garney's parents, particularly his father, supported his decision to turn down a relatively secure and lucrative offer to pursue his dreams. Both his parents had different reasons for their support. For Maggie, it was geography. For his father, it had somewhat to do with both he and his eldest son following him, opting not to choose the possible professional sports careers available to them. Stephen Senior suggested that his youngest son should follow his dream for a two-year time frame to establish himself in the industry. He warned Garney that his cash flow would depend on the whims of his club members and their desire for lessons or new equipment. This concept was not lost on Garney as he knew many golf club members and amateur golfers were turning to the large golf box stores for their equipment, their shoes, their lessons, and their clothing. Golf merchandise was becoming a very competitive business. It was difficult for the small golf pro shops to compete on the larger ticket items. Coach Patterson and Garney's mentor and friend George offered an alternative to Garney. They suggested that he probably could take a slightly different path than the one he had chosen. He should attempt to participate in some competitive golf. Obtaining a professional PGA card was a long, arduous route. One with obstacles and challenging times, but the rewards for those who were successful were monumental. It was a long shot at best for even seasoned PGA veterans who had not earned enough money during the previous season to stay on tour. They failed to maintain their full playing card by not finishing in the top 125 players on the tour. Swamp stated, "You may not become as successful financially, but I am certain you will be happy. Your decision may or may not lead to a career. As you know, there are many capable young players found on the golf courses in this country. They all have picture-perfect swings and the ability to strike a golf ball long and accurately. You won't be unique. However, I feel if you don't try, it might always bother you. Only you will determine if you are one of the players who have that something special that sets true professional golfers apart."

# Chapter 32: Joining The Tour

In addition to the well-known PGA tour, there were several minor playing tours and satellite tours. These serve as stepping stones to a career playing for a living as a top tour golf professional. Another method of obtaining a PGA playing card was by having success in the demanding week-long Qualifying School, a series of tournaments that eliminated many during the play along the way. To the aspirants, it was felt to be the most heart-wrenching experience of their lives. The pressure they faced while advancing or falling aside during the qualifying, zone, and regional tournaments was cruel. The player's next few years would depend on their ability and the breaks and, in a number of cases, some luck during the Q school week. For some, luck favored them. For others, it broke their heart. A favorable bounce off a tree, the weather that is good in the morning but poor in the afternoon, a putt that went around but not in the hole. Factors that were beyond their control. Q-school tested prospective players to determine who among them had nerves of steel.

The taste of the trials was palpable and, in many cases, heartbreaking. Cotton or dry mouth was a common condition both on and off the course for those attempting to qualify in the "Q".

Many had left their jobs, spent their life savings, borrowed from friends and family, and slept in cars and campers while traveling to the regional and zone qualifying tournaments. Others who were better prepared financially were able to sleep fitfully in one of the many chains of familiar motels that seemed to be found on the outskirts of America's towns and cities. There was one common denominator: all of the contestants could play the game of golf at a very high level. They were known in the golfing world as flat bellies. It is worth considering that only fifteen percent of America's golfers can shoot a score below one hundred on a regular basis. These competing golfers were all able to post scores near or below par almost every time that they teed the ball up. They were the lowest percentile scorers in the game of golf. These golfers also played much longer courses than the general population. They were good! These aspiring golfers came with various pedigrees, ages, and backgrounds. The majority were clones in their twenties, flat-bellied, athletic, with similar smooth swings. They were used to being the best players in their group and their local areas. The difference seemed to be mental toughness and good fortune. A putt deflected by a spike mark, an excellent drive finding a divot in an otherwise carpet-like fairway, Mother Nature and the pressure had jumped up and crushed the dreams of many prospective professional PGA card holders. Those who seemed to be unfairly punished returned to lesser playing tours or other occupations in mainstream America. The Holy Grail was out of reach for many each year.

During a conversation with the Foster family, George Trent suggested that if Garney was to qualify and play at some tour level, sponsorship of some sort was necessary. He would need some financial support to survive an initial year of competition. In his early days, George recalled having to leave his goal on a mini tour to replenish his coffers by seeking temporary employment. George even hustled local players by betting for money at municipal courses where he was unknown, and this was a sometimes dangerous practice. In his first three years of competitive golf, this happened regularly. George knew that a golfer couldn't compete if his mind was preoccupied with his wallet's contents or lack thereof. Expenses for entry fees, golf balls and equipment, travel, and day-to-day expenses such as meals and accommodations had to be considered. Corporate sponsorship from the golf industry was reserved for those who had already arrived and competed in one of the top tours. They received logoed equipment and clothing gratis to become walking billboards. Golf manufacturers seemed to provide the well-known PGA players with more equipment and clothing than they could ever use. The friends and family of the regular pros on the big tour usually played gratis with the newest styles and best equipment each year. The struggling pros that seemed to need help the most were at the lower end of the corporate manufacturers' pecking order for free equipment and clothing. In almost all cases, prospective professional golfers had to provide for themselves on the mini-tours.

This was not an easy way to earn a living for new young professionals trying to rise to the next level. The prize money was fairly substantial, but after two days of a four-day tournament, more than half of the field was eliminated and received no remuneration for that event. They were leaving with what they arrived with as a reward for their efforts. On to the next event, no cash flow, just expenses.

On the plus side, Garney was single, educated, and had just completed four years of independence. He was accustomed to fast foods and a somewhat transient lifestyle. He had traveled with his college golf team and stayed in motels near other colleges and universities. He was accustomed to playing unfamiliar golf courses, and he had learned to cut corners and expenses. Garney was not a spendthrift, and on some occasions, when there was no iron or ironing board available in the motel room, he would press his golf slacks at night between the mattress and the box spring of his bed.

The young man was grounded in a solid family and had honed his golf skills to a highly competitive level. George Trent and Dave Patterson had every confidence that this young golfer could be successful immediately on one of the satellite tours. Playing there would serve as a grooming ground for more advanced tours and, hopefully, eventually, the PGA tour. They both felt he had something special. Foster's Hardware, Grant's Chev-Old's car dealership, and Birch Run Golf and Country Club became one-year sponsors for the aspiring golf professional Garney Foster. That summer, Garney became an assistant pro at "Birch Run," and he prepared diligently for the task ahead. With his savings and sponsorship, he had the essential travel, food, and accommodation finances. Any prize money that he might earn would be a bonus.

# Chapter 33: Turning Pro

The mini-tour began. Garney started the golf season in the state of North Carolina. Another two aspiring golfers he had met, one through college golf, the other at a PGA qualifying school, would travel with him. They would share the common expenses of accommodation, gas, and some meals. Dale Goff was from Lakeland, Florida, and had attended the University of Florida in Gainesville. He was a Florida Gator. He received his golf training on several public courses in the Lakeland area. The other member of the group was Tom Pennington, a Canadian who had been golfing in amateur competitions throughout North America. Like many Canadian golfers, Tom played the game left-handed. It was believed that playing hockey contributed to swinging from the port side for many Canadian golfers. The percentage of lefthanded golfers in Canada was much higher than that of those in the United States. All three of their group were among many exceptional young golfers attempting to make a living playing a game that most players struggle with on courses worldwide.

Dale owned a new Dodge Caravan with ample space for three young men, their luggage, golf clubs, and other paraphernalia. Dale came from a family that owned a successful car dealership in central Florida. The threesome would book two connecting hotel rooms and alternately rotate the use of the single room every third week. This enabled the young men to each have a chance for some private time every third week.

The tour began in Raleigh, North Carolina, and was hosted by the Old Chatham Golf Course. Garney had flown in from Detroit, and Dale and Tom met him at terminal two of the Raleigh International Airport. This was the first tournament in a season of mini-tour tournaments. Most of these competitions were played in an area that stretched from Florida to Texas and as far north as Virginia. Other tournament stops in many of the southern states would fill out the schedule.

Old Chatham Course turned out to be one of the better courses that they would play that season. Over six days, practice at the driving range and the putting green was held on Monday, registration and one practice round on Tuesday, and four days of competition starting Thursday became a routine. Wednesdays were usually set aside for obligatory pro-amateur events with amateur golfers and local celebrities participating. The tournament golf play began with assigned morning or afternoon tee times and was held on Thursdays and Fridays, depending on the draw and player's rankings. Saturday and Sunday were only for those who scored low enough to make the cut. About half of the field qualified for the cut for the weekend. Those that failed to do so were eliminated from further play. Elimination was referred to as a "trunk slammer" by those who left for the next tournament early. Not making the cut led to an early departure by way of the Eisenhower Interstate Expressway system for the competition in the next scheduled city.

The purses were generally small when compared to the PGA tour, and winning even one of these tournaments paid for a decent amount of travel and living expenses for the balance of the season. In the hierarchy of professional golf, these mini-tournaments would be considered to be a level three or four. The level one PGA televised events had millions of dollars of prize money. This did not include all the financial perks for players at the top of the competitions. Endorsements, appearance fees, and adulation made all the "A" player's multimillionaires. Level two was the next step to this nirvana. The Korn Ferry tour, previously known under other names, was considered a level two, just below the PGA, and it was the final launching pad for entry to the "big show." Professional golfers at all four levels were capable of breaking par and shooting low scores. Having experience was the final necessary ingredient to becoming a household name. Steps up the ladder take time, and some never master the first few rungs. Sponsorship and some prize money at the entry level enabled some to follow their dream. Some carried a burden of feeling they must earn some money for the sponsors or themselves. This pressure could drastically affect their game. Additional pressure is placed on aspiring young professionals unnecessarily.

By sharing expenses at the onset of the tour, Dale, Tom, and Garney were able to live decently. All three had some sponsorship from friends and family. They stayed in the better-class motels and tended to eat at decent restaurants. This was supplemented by some fast food on occasion. No steady peanut butter and jam diet was necessary to sustain these young men. A decent breakfast usually came with their hotel accommodations. They discussed the possibility of sharing and dividing their prize money. The player who won the most prize money that week retained a bit more than the other two. They developed a formula that rewarded the larger money winner the lion's share each week.

The golfing participants provided the prize money at level three tournaments. The entry fee was usually $500 to $600 with a field of about eighty to one hundred golfers. Total purses of $50,000 were common. Only about a third of the field would cash in for some of the prize money. The cash awards were top-heavy, with the winner receiving the largest share, the remaining top five finishers doing reasonably well, and the remainder of the top third qualifiers winning back more than their entry fee. Level three mini-tours are a great place to gain experience and learn how to handle an abundance of pressure. As the year proceeds, with fewer tournaments remaining and with money going out and none coming in, the problem of squeezing their golf grip becomes the norm for some of the less fortunate.

# Chapter 34: Connie

It was their very first Saturday evening on the tour. Garney and Tom had failed to make the cut after Thursday and Friday play over the first two days. Dale qualified and had just finished his third round on Saturday. The threesome had returned to spend the night in their hotel. It was dinner time. The choice was between a burger franchise or a restaurant catering to North Carolina State's university crowd. They opted for the college restaurant.

The establishment was decked out in sports paraphernalia, with the predominant colors being red and more red and white. Over the bar was a gigantic picture of Jim Valvano, the renowned basketball coach, shirt tails flying, racing onto the basketball floor after North Carolina State had just won the NCAA Division 1 basketball championship.

There were four apparent coeds sitting at a nearby table. The girls were doing their best to make a connection with the three young men. Tom, Dale, and Garney eventually returned the flirting. After finishing their meals, the two groups joined each other in the restaurant parking lot. After an introductory conversation, they all agreed to have a drink at another nearby bar. Three of the young girls were students at the university, while the fourth was a friend of one of the coeds. The friend was visiting from West Virginia, and her name was Connie. This young lady seemed particularly infatuated with Garney, and it became very evident that she had him in her crosshairs. Earlier that evening, Garney had been the deciding vote as to where they would have dinner that night. One vote for fast food, and one vote for the restaurant. Garney was the deciding choice. It was a decision that would haunt him and one that he would regret for a long time. It began his biggest nightmare.

Over the next two hours. Connie made it very obvious she wanted more of Garney. She eventually asked to meet and walk the golf course on Sunday with him when he followed Dale on Dale's final round of golf at the tournament. Tom would join them. On Sunday, as they followed Dale's finishing round of golf, her questions were non-stop, and Garney was vague at best with his answers. He wanted to reveal as little as possible. Her curious behavior concerned him. Also, she was not Carley. Attractive enough but not nearly as beautiful. It also reminded him that Carley lived somewhere here in the Carolinas.

At the end of the day, Dale had finished in fifth place and earned a cheque for $1850. It was a good start for his young professional career. As per agreement with his roommates, he would keep $1350, and they would split the remaining $500. This agreement would surely balance out over the season as each was capable of earning money on any given week.

Connie asked to see Garney again that night, but he quickly advised her that their van was already packed, as they had checked out of their hotel that morning. They were on their way to the next city, a 180-mile trip to the next event.

"Where are you going next?" she asked. Garney wanted to lie, but the schedule was on the internet for everyone to Google, so he stated, "The next tournament was near Myrtle Beach." He had an ominous feeling that he didn't want her to know where it was scheduled. With all the golf courses, chain motels, and hotels in the area, he had a feeling they would be safe.

Dale placed his clubs in the back of the van. In a show of pride, he kissed his monetary cheque earnings, and after goodbyes, they parted for the "Beach." The Dodge pulled out of the golf course parking lot and its entrance laneway, with Tom driving and Garney riding shotgun. Dale glanced back to see a yellow Volkswagen Beetle a few car lengths behind them. It seemed to be traveling on the very same path.

"Isn't that Connie's car? "Dale asked as they turned onto the south ramp to the expressway. The yellow bug was following not far behind. "I thought she was going north to Beckley. That's where she said she is from, wasn't it?"

Garney responded, "I sure hope it's not her. She is scary. The last we see of her, I hope. If I never see her again, it'll be too soon." Unknown to them, other people in her past had always felt this girl's living room lights seemed on, but it didn't appear that anyone was home.

Tom said, "Don't worry, she's a little weird but not shit-bat crazy." The other two chuckled and thought that this must be a Canadian expression.

However, this was the beginning of torment and horror from hell for this young man and his family from Michigan. Garney's uneasy feeling and his instinct told him maybe he should worry. As it turned out, his instinct was spot on. Garney wished he could be a little more like Bo. Bo would have screwed her and then told her to fuck off. That was not in Garney's character, even though they were raised in the same household by the same parents.

It was a typical summer-like evening as they wound their way south on Interstate Ninety-Five. Twenty minutes later, when he looked back, Dale could faintly make out several cars in a group. The pack included a yellow vehicle. Being concerned, Garney searched for an alternate route to their destination by using his cell phone's Google Maps. He wanted to try to ensure that they were not being followed. A slower alternative coastal highway appeared a few miles ahead. Garney urged Tom to pick up the pace a bit to the turnoff exit. Tom increased the speed and joined the alternate route unnoticed by the vehicles following them. It was a slower route, but all of them, especially Garney, felt some relief as they continued their travels to South Carolina.

# Chapter 35: FIRST SNAFU

In due time, the threesome eventually arrived at their next hotel, the second of many on their golfing journey. Tom went ahead of the others, entered the hotel, and crossed the lobby to the front desk. It was Tom's turn in their rotation to register for their adjoining rooms. It was also Tom's turn to have the single room as per their arrangement and their schedule. With the single room came the job of registering for their stay. Dale and Garney had found a luggage cart and were placing the suitcases and clubs on the cart.

Tom returned to the vehicle and frustratingly stated, "You won't believe what the hell is going on. The desk clerk said Mrs. Foster had already registered and was up in one of the suites with the keys waiting for us."

Garney felt nauseous, and his golfing buddies were not feeling much better. There was no Mrs. Foster. Dale asked Tom if he had paid yet or had left his credit card at the desk. Tom quickly responded no, he had not. In unison, they all exclaimed in one form or another, let's get the hell out of here. We should be able to find another hotel or motel on the strip. Using the phone number, he spotted on the large "Renaissance Motel" sign, Garney called the hotel desk to cancel their rooms while the other two reloaded the van. When the clerk started to explain that cancellation was impossible due to the room already being occupied.

Garney told the clerk to "call the cops. We don't know her; she is not anybody's wife. I am sorry for the inconvenience; goodbye." There was an urgency to leave as quickly as possible before they were sighted by the "shit-bat" crazy woman. They had discovered and begun to use the now newly familiar Canadian phrase.

Fortunately, the area was an array of hotels, motels, and golf courses. The only prerequisite was they had to have parking that was not visible from the road. After a short search, their conditions were met, and Tom registered in a hotel with underground parking. Tom had the single room, and Garney and Dale shared the other connecting room. It was a Sunday evening, and they all felt safer ordering some food up to their room. None of the young golfers decided to leave their rooms that evening.

Dale asked for a meeting to discuss this "stupid goddamn situation." While waiting for their pizza delivery, they began discussing their dilemma. Dale started, "We are only just starting, and it's becoming a cluster-fuck. This was our first tournament, Garney. I don't want to play hide and seek and try to become a touring pro under these conditions. It could be my future." Catching himself, he added, "Our futures, I should say."

"Garney, you have to fix this, or we will have to make other arrangements. This is horrible. I know it's not even close to your fault," stated Tom. "But it's not our fault either. Both Dale and I are caught up in this mess as well."

"Garney, you gotta speak to the cops or the tournament organizers. We have to live somewhat normally to try to compete. She has to go! I don't want to play hide and seek for 20 weeks. As much as I hate to say it, we solve this, or we end the plans we have as a trio." Dale was getting hot.

Garney had not spoken a word as he didn't know where to begin. "OK, I don't want to call home for advice, so I have to solve this without terrifying my mom and dad. I could call Brother Bo, and he would send her packing, but he is so….."

With that, there was a knock on the door, and three strapping and physically fit men bolted to their feet. A hundred-and-twenty-pound young female had three very fit 180-pound athletes almost leaping out of their skin. As Garney approached the door, Dale whispered, "Don't open it."

Garney looked through the peephole and said under his breath, "I think it's her. What do we do?"

"Look again to make sure," whispered Tom. After a second, more thorough look, Garney replied, "No, it's not. It's not the same color hair, but she has a pizza jacket on, and she looks heavier." A peephole distorted images, creating a slightly different appearance from those outside in the hall.

Since they had prepaid for their food on the internet and included the tip, Dale asked the delivery girl to "just leave it outside, and thanks."

To be safe, Tom went to the adjoining room and peeked out the hall door. The coast was clear. No one was to be seen in either direction. The young golfers wondered if the stalker had a gun and if she was capable of using it. This couldn't become the normal routine behavior for the trio. It was starting to be possible that any one or all of their professional golf futures, or even worse, were at risk. This was particularly true in Garney's case. As far as meals went, they didn't want to eat in their rooms regularly. Pizza and Chinese food get old in a hurry.

# Chapter 36: Frankie?

Myrtle Beach is known as a golf mecca with courses and packages for all abilities. It is a huge tourist attraction for families and golf enthusiasts alike. Garney decided to approach the organizers about the stalking problem.

When they arrived at the Burning Ridge Golf Club golf course, Garney headed for the pro shop and offices, where he hoped to find a sympathetic ear. He spent some time explaining his dilemma but to no avail. No help was provided.

After his plea, he returned to the practice putting green, where Dale and Tom were in conversation with a few other tour golfers. They were fellow golfers they had recognized and competed against during the first tournament in Raleigh. They were all practicing their putting, probably the most essential part of the golf game. "Drive for show and putt for dough" was a jingle well-known among all levels of golfers.

Garney joined the group, and introductions were made. One of the putting competitors stated to Garney, "Good to meet you, Garney. See you hooked up with the skank. Better you than any of us."

"Who is the skank?" asked the young tour rookie.

"Frankie, she is from Ohio or Indiana or West Virginia. Out here, she is called Frank the skank." She is older than she looks and has been hanging around this tour for three or four years. We think her goal is to eventually latch on to a golfer who can make it to the main PGA tour. She has a huge ego. She wants to get on television so that when her man wins on the PGA, she can trot out to the eighteenth green and give him a big hug. Word of warning: stay away; we think she might be dangerous; you know what they say about a woman scorned."

Garney replied, "First, she was introduced to us as Connie. Second, I want nothing to do with her. Third, I think I am being stalked. Fourth, she said she is from West Virginia. Lastly, I just spoke to the organizers, and they said it sounds like a police matter. They cannot ban people from attending and watching the tournament. I doubt the police would take this very seriously. I think she is already somewhere in town. She caused us to find a different hotel last night."

Another member of the group offered. "Tell her if she does show up to take a hike, nothing is happening here. Tell her you are married or engaged."

Garney replied, "I can only hope it's that easy. I am trying to put my mind on golf, not on some dingbat's whereabouts. I was looking forward to doing this tour, at least for this stage of my life. I missed the first cut in the opening tournament, and now this crap. Tom and Dale, my travel partners here, are also affected by her. It's not fair to them either."

Another member of the group added that she had caused a young golfer to quit the tour after a few events the previous season. She had left her mark. He had a nervous breakdown and hadn't earned a dime or made a cut before he left for home.

The groups parted, and they left the golf course. Garney and his friends decided to locate a Roadhouse restaurant to have some lunch. Dale suggested that "maybe we can come back later to the driving range or the putting green. We can get our minds back where they belong."

As they left the course, Garney felt better. Perhaps he was making something out of nothing. A mountain out of a molehill. This would probably all go away. How wrong he was.

# Chapter 37: Myrtle Beach

The following day led to the Tuesday practice round for all of the entrants. Garney liked the appearance and the physical layout of this week's course. During these 18 practice holes, he played his "A" game and scored very well. Better still, there was no sign of Connie or Frankie or whoever the hell she was.

That night's sleep was fitful as he imagined that tomorrow, on the Wednesday pro-am, a member of his amateur four-some would be Connie or Frankie, his stalker. To participate in the pro-am, an amateur only had to pay a reasonably expensive entry fee. Knowing someone involved in the tournament's organization or being a member of the golf course would help as well. Unbeknownst to him, the 'Skank' knew someone involved in the tournament's organization.

The following morning, on the tournament's pro-am day, he and Dale were up early and starting to get organized for breakfast. Dale opened the connecting door between the rooms, and looking into Tom's room, he saw that both beds had been slept in. He could hear that Tom was in the shower. That's odd, thought Dale. Why would he use both beds?

Later, when he was questioned, Tom was unaware that the other bed had been used.

127

Tom had wondered what a tube of lipstick was doing beside the sink. "That's what sound sleep will do to you. Shit, I never heard a thing. What the hell, how would someone get in here?"

Garney found a note next to the pillow on Tom's extra bed in the adjoining room: "See you at the course. All My Love." Garney's stomach turned, and he felt ill again. It wasn't going to end quickly.

The motel breakfast was soon finished. Even though most free hotel breakfasts were substantial, they certainly were not gourmet. The best part was they were handy, filling, and free, which also fit their budgets nicely. The van was then loaded with their golf clubs, and they began their drive to this week's golf tournament. The drive to Burning Ridge was short, and soon, they had arrived in the club parking lot. Their entry fee had been paid shortly after arriving, and they were registered at the sign-in desk. Registration would take a little longer as all the participants arrived simultaneously. Tom said we should learn from this and pre-register at the Tuesday practice rounds. Things were starting to have a familiar feel. Most of the competitors' faces were recognizable from the previous week's tournament. Garney attempted to settle down, and he headed for the driving range. He wanted to have his golf warm-up, which included a few practice swings and a few practice shots.

He was introduced to his amateur playing partners as his tee time approached. The three players in his group were a local businessman, a golfing tourist who was a late entry substitution for a no-show, and a businesswoman. They were all very nice people. The game was a better ball format, with the amateurs using their appropriate handicaps and tee boxes. After the front nine, their team was scoring very well, and they were probably amongst the leading groups. The three men were very fortunate, as luck would have it; the female golfer in their foursome was a very low handicap player. She had won two holes with a net birdie on each of the holes. She also saved the team on a challenging par four by scoring with a regular par while the three men, including Garney, bogeyed the hole. The back nine was very similar, and at the end of the day, the team found themselves in third position in the field. After a stand-up luncheon with some socializing and prizes for the guests, everyone departed and headed for the parking lot. It had turned out to be a pleasant pro-am day.

There, parked in the lot, standing all by itself, was a yellow Volkswagen with Ohio plates. A good day was ruined. Where in the hell was she, and what was she doing? For that matter, where was she from? Ohio plates?

# Chapter 38: The Room Key

Later, when they returned and entered the lobby, Garney approached the desk and explained their awkward situation. Someone had access to their room and, unknowingly to them, had slept in the spare bed in one of their two rooms last night. He gave the desk clerk their suspicions as to who it was and wondered how she could have received a key. The desk clerk appeared shocked. He asked if any of them were aware of the interloper. He apologized and assured me that night security would take special note of the incident and be more vigilant tonight and in the future. No other room keys would be issued, and could they please exchange their original plastic card room keys before they returned to their rooms?

The clerk stated he was changing the lock code as they spoke. The desk clerk stated that they would not be charged for their first night's stay. As an afterthought, he asked if they would like to change rooms. The trio politely declined the offer. The clerk then asked for a description of the lady. Garney immediately described the yellow Volkswagen with Ohio or West Virginia tags. He briefly described Connie or Frankie, then suggested that the police should be called for her trespassing or breaking and entering. The clerk said he would give it some consideration and he would call the local police to explain the situation.

# Chapter 39: Three Amigos

The first two days of the tournament play occurred without any further incident, although Garney was ever aware of who was in his surroundings. He was constantly on the alert for someone shadowing him. The swings in a golf tournament's results are ever-changing, and after the two-day cut, both Tom and Garney had qualified for that weekend's play and a possible paycheck. Dale had missed the cut by one stroke and became one of that tournament's 'trunk slammers." Each group member taking turns missing the cut during the season would continue this way. Only four times did all three golfers manage to make the cut and play on the same weekend. There was one tournament in Louisiana where none of them, who had become to be known by their competitors as the 'three amigos,' survived the cut. When that occurred, they left Shreveport, Louisiana, on a Saturday morning, heading for the next destination on the tour two days early.

# Chapter 40: Yellow Volkswagen

In Myrtle Beach, after Saturday's round of golf, Tom's and Garney's last names, Pennington and Foster, were posted on the large leaderboard near the clubhouse. They were tied for the fourth spot, only two shots behind the leader when the front nine had been completed. Both continued to play a strong back nine, and they finished their day tied for second place, only three shots behind the leader. The two amigos would be in the same threesome on the final day of the tournament. That evening, before calling it a day and heading for bed, Garney looked out their third-floor window, and there it was. The yellow Volkswagen was parked below, only half a dozen parking spaces from the hotel entrance. She was still around. She was nearby. It gave the young golfer a weird and ominous feeling. He had a knot in his stomach.

On Sunday morning, at the golf club for the final day's play, one of the participants whom they had met earlier at the putting green said, "Garney, I see your girlfriend is here."

"Where?" Garney blurted out, "She is not my anything. She's a royal pain in the ass. She's a nut case."

"She's just over there, near the scorekeeper's table. Oops, she is gone now. She was just there a minute ago." Her presence made the young man extremely alert, and he felt concerned. How was it going to affect his play in the final round? He was correct as he tumbled down the leaderboard while Tom continued scrambling and remained in contention during this final round.

Midway through the back nine on the fourteenth hole, Frankie finally made an appearance. Garney was preparing to hit his approach shot to the putting surface. After hitting a very good drive to the middle of the fairway, he was now only one hundred and twenty yards to the flag. An easy pitching wedge would be his club of choice, and he struck the ball firmly. Following the ball's flight, he could see it was probably his best shot that round so far. As the ball descended toward the flag pin, a loud female voice yelled, "That's my man, Garney." There she was, standing behind the green with a handful of other spectators. His worst nightmare was here.

As they walked toward the green, Tom, who was playing in the same group that day, moved to walk alongside him. Tom said, "Ignore her. Just make the putt. It looks like it's only a six-footer for the bird." Garney noticed Dale, who had been following them during the play, had stormed to the back of the green and, in an animated conversation with Frankie, directed her to get lost. What he yelled was, "Fuck off". Dale was so enraged that he quickly made his point, and Frankie departed the area with no argument. Two male spectators started to confront Dale but realized that it would be best not to poke the bear at that point and moved away.

Garney finished the round with no further damage but with a lump in his stomach. Garney had begun the day tied for fourth and finished the day in twelfth position, good enough to receive his entry fee as his prize money. Tom played steadily and took home second place and a prize worth eighty thousand eight hundred dollars. Once again, the group was ahead of the game financially but starting to fray as a group after only two events.

The Dodge Caravan had already been packed and was in the golf club parking lot. Soon, their drive to the next competition was underway. They had developed their routine. Firstly, to check out of the motel in the morning before driving to the event's final round of the competition. This would save them a night's hotel bill and give them an earlier arrival at the next tournament. This was always well before they had to register for the next event and prepare at the golf course for the next stop in their schedule.

This also gave them a free day. It enabled them to get settled into their next accommodation and to get a general feel for the new city. It was time to locate the golf course and get the lay of the land.

The yellow Volkswagen was nowhere to be seen in the parking lot as they departed Myrtle Beach for Augusta. As they traveled, Garney was accustomed to being ever vigilant for any sign of a yellow Volkswagen. It wasn't unusual for any yellow vehicle to catch his attention, and he often reacted viscerally.

# Chapter 41: Augusta

It was now Sunday evening, and Garney and Tom were settled in their motel room in a Holiday Inn. They were in Augusta, Georgia, for the tour's third leg. Dale left the room and went down to the parking area to tidy the inside of his van. He removed the packaging, cups, and napkins from the seats and floor. It was his van, and he was somewhat fastidious, which had already become evident to the other two. Each day, he reorganized his golf bag and washed his clubs. Garney respected fastidious. Tom, not so much. Tom already had to replace one of his wedges. He had lost it at one of the first two events. Fortunately, Tom was able to find a nearly exact replacement at a large Dicks Golf Store in Myrtle Beach. From Myrtle Beach, it had been a drive of about two hundred and twenty miles and almost four and a half hours in duration. This included time for a quick drive-thru dinner at a national burger chain. Dale returned to the room, and it was now ten thirty p.m. All three, exhausted, were pleased to turn in for the night. Tomorrow, on an off day, they will look for this week's venue, Forest Hills Golf Course.

On a Monday morning, they routinely opted to locate their course with the van's GPS. It turned out to be a very brief drive of less than four miles. As a reprieve from golfing, the three decided they would try to locate the famous Augusta National Golf Club of "Masters" tournament renown. They held some hope they might be able to see some of the renowned golf course. Unfortunately, it is closed to the public, and no amount of cajoling and explaining that they were golf professionals would gain them entrance to look at the prestigious property.

Later that afternoon, back at their hotel, Garney decided to go down to the hotel exercise room to use the treadmill and ride the stationary bike. Tom was lying down reading a novel, and Dale was practicing putting on the carpet in the hall corridor. He felt putts had been his downfall in the past Myrtle Beach event. As Garney exited the elevator and entered the lobby, a female at the desk who was checking in caught his eye. "God damn," it was her.

Garney immediately decided to confront this problem face-on before he lost his nerve. He strode quickly and forcefully across the lobby, loudly and aggressively stating that he wanted to speak to her when she was finished.

Connie retorted, "At long last, you realize we have to talk to each other; you finally understand our need to be together." The clerk quickly interrupted and asked, "Is everything all right, miss? Do you need any assistance?"

Connie or Frankie said, "Thank you. Everything is just fine. It was kind of you to ask." Garney and Frankie then found a quiet seating area some distance from the desk.

Garney began the conversation. "I am a married man, and I love my wife, so please understand I do not want to be involved with another woman."

Frankie first admitted, "Frankie is my name, and your nose is growing when you tell me things like that. I know a lot more about you than you are aware. I am not going to accept your lies. How is your cat, Wedgy? Are you looking forward to seeing her?" After a pause, "Is your older brother Steve still getting married?"

The hair on the young man's neck and arms stood up. He thought, Jesus Christ, what the fuck am I dealing with? "How do you know that?" he replied.

"I know just about everything, at least all I need to know for now. How is George? How long did you work for him? Do you miss Carley?"

This was something out of a Stephen King novel, and Garney mused that this was scaring the crap out of him. "Who are you? Why are you doing this to me? I don't know you, who are you?"

"All you need to know for now is I am Frankie, and I am the daughter of a very, very powerful wealthy man. I wish I had known that you boys wanted to see the Augusta golf course. I could have got you in. I saw you, you know."

With that, Garney stated, "I am asking you nicely, please leave me alone; my focus is becoming a golfer, and I don't have time for a relationship, particularly with someone I know nothing about."

"Is it the sex? I am great in the sack. I almost woke up Tommy the other night and gave myself to him to see if that would make you jealous."

"If this doesn't stop now, I am going to involve the police. This can't continue. This is insane," Garney blurted out.

"Go ahead, call the cops. I have a witness." Frankie stated.

Garney said, "What witness, witness for what?"

"The desk clerk saw the way you were aggressive and shouting at me."

"Bullroar, I just said I wanted to talk to you. Could you stay away from me? That's it. I am outta here. Leave me alone." With that, Garney stormed off.

As he entered the elevator, he heard, "See you later, sweetheart."

# Chapter 42: Phone Home

Garney knew he had to phone his parents later that evening, but he was visibly upset. He had to relax and settle down before he called home. Garney had continued to maintain a connection with his parents in Michigan, but thus far, only by email. He knew they would want to talk with him personally, and that evening, he had to oblige. It was his turn this weekend to have the single room, and he would be able to talk privately for as long as he wished. His golf information would be up to date, and they would know how he was doing on the tour; statistics were available on the Internet. However, they would want to know the details, especially his mother, Maggie. Was he eating properly? How were his roommates? Was the weather holding up? Did he need anything? Did he miss Wedge? Had he been talking to Bo in Ypsilanti at Eastern Michigan? Are you taking care of your money? Will he be able to miss an event and fly home for a few days? Just hearing the sound of their voices would be wonderful. Garney missed Michigan more than he wanted to admit. Garney was worried that his mother, in particular, would detect any strain in his voice. Mothers always knew. He had to be sure to sound confident. The last thing that he wanted to do was divulge the escapades of the loose cannon that was stalking his every move. He would phone them later that evening. It gave him some time to settle down. Garney told Dale and Tom that he had something to discuss with them later that evening.

Garney and his parents had a wonderful conversation that evening. The young man felt comfortable that his mother had not sensed that he was having any difficulty. He was correct in surmising what questions she would ask. Garney only missed the one regarding Wedge. Stephen Senior quizzed him on his golf game and whether he needed any help. The way his father inquired about needing help was odd. Strangely, it seemed that his father had twigged that something seemed amiss. Father's intuition? Was there such a thing? Was it Garney's voice? Once again, a little paranoia was creeping into his thoughts.

Later that evening, Garney, Tom, and Dale reluctantly discussed the huge problem that confronted him earlier in the hotel lobby. Garney spared no detail and how much in control but how deranged Frankie seemed. He was aware that when he described what had just occurred, he was jeopardizing his traveling arrangement with his golfing partners. Tom and Dale, much to young Foster's relief, agreed to give this situation a bit more time. They didn't want to leave their new roommate without any support. Previously, Dale had stated to Tom, "Let's try to put ourselves in his shoes and ride this problem out for a while. It wasn't affecting our earnings nor our golf very much."

# Chapter 43: Visiting Masters

Augusta National is the most exclusive and famous golf course in North America, perhaps the world. It is also the home of the Masters. However, this was obviously not listed on the player's mini-tour itinerary.

Golf membership at Augusta National is the home of the wealthy and powerful. The course is closed each summer from the months of May to October. The temperature and humidity during that time of the year made it far too uncomfortable to play golf. It was the closest these three mini-tour players would come to playing there. They would have to move through the ranks and up the rungs of the following two tours. They would have to earn their PGA playing card. This would be a necessary requisite for an entry to the Masters Tournament. They would then require some additional combination or formula of victories and points for an invitation.

Augusta was also known for many other exquisite golf properties. The tour this week was to be played at the Forest Hills Golf Club, home of the Augusta NCAA University Jaguars, the 2010 NCAA golf champions. The history of the relationship of Augusta with the famed golfer Bobby Jones is legendary.

This tournament was like the others held during the previous two weeks. It was starting to feel similar. The third mini-tour event included the same pressures as those in Raleigh and Myrtle Beach. It's the same as trying not to shoot yourself in the foot, playing safe when necessary, and taking chances when the risk reward is in your favor.

There were a few sightings of Frankie over the next four days, but she maintained her distance. With her appearance, Frankie made sure to let the group know she had not disappeared. Her presence was likened to 'waiting to hear the other shoe drop.'

Everything appeared quite normal when the practice rounds, the pro-am, and four days of competition had concluded. For the first time, all 'three amigos' had received a pay cheque for their good play. Tom and Garney returned their entry fees, and Dale cashed a fourth-place finish of nearly $7500. They were three of the better golfers on this mini-tour. There seemed to be an abundance of what were called flat bellies. Young, fit men with good golf backgrounds and the ability to hit most golf shots required to be successful. Length off the tee was not a problem for most of them. 300-yard drives had become quite common. Improvements in nutrition, fitness, and equipment played a significant role in a positive change in the caliber of play. As courses were becoming too short and at the mercy of many upper-level golfers, something had to be done. At the highest PGA level, winning scores of 20 or more under par for a tournament were the rule rather than the exception. The winner often averaged four or five under par for four consecutive days. Established courses were running out of property to create more length for the professional golf tours. Various groups proffered solutions, and the answer most often reached was to change the equipment that was being used. Change the golf ball to a larger or smaller ball and change the golf club. An argument that had been heard and discussed over the last decade or two.

The threesome had decent results in the tournament and, once again, turned a profit. Fortunately, Frankie was not seen again in Augusta.

# Chapter 44: Elvis

Now, on to the next venue in Brunswick, Georgia, which was a three-and-a-half-hour drive; the driving had been tolerable to this point as all three had taken their turns behind the wheel. They had a rotation where each young man enjoyed his turn in the back seat during the trips. As they departed Augusta about four that Sunday afternoon, they expected to be in their rooms in Brunswick by eight o'clock, still enough time to go out for dinner. The trip was uneventful as the scenery changed from the Georgia pines to the intercostal waterway scenery with innumerable marshes and inlets.

About 7:30 p.m., the van pulled into the parking lot of the Hampton Inn and Suites. Dale headed for the lobby area to register for their weeklong stay. Once again, Garney started to unload their luggage and their golf clubs, and Tom set out to find a luggage cart. This was a rotation they had developed and followed. The routine was based on the person whose turn it was for the single room.

When Dale approached the room clerk, he found himself alone at the counter. "A reservation for Goff and party," he stated. The clerk turned to his computer and, a few moments later, said, "Sir, you canceled that reservation yesterday."

"No, no, no, there was no cancellation; that's a mistake. No one canceled. It has been reserved for about ten weeks."

"I am sorry, sir, but we received a cancellation. If you check your credit card, there should be a reversed entry there in a few days. We have no other rooms available. I am afraid to say the city is fully booked for this coming week. Our area is holding an annual Elvis Festival, and there is a golf tournament as well. People come from miles away to compete and attend both events. I think you will have a difficult time getting any room within sixty miles of here."

At that moment, Tom and Garney rolled up with a full cart of baggage. Clubs were awkward and stuck out on both sides. Tom was busy pushing clubs back into golf bags. Garney asked, "Is there something wrong?" to anyone who would respond.

Dale said, "She screwed us up again; she canceled our reservation. There's nothing here and apparently nothing for sixty miles. Shit, shit, shit, shit, shit."

Tom piped up, "I've had it, I'll kick her ass, I'd like to smack her in the face."

With eyebrows raised, the clerk stated, "I can see you're in the golf tournament, right."

The three responded, "Yes," in unison. The clerk, according to his name tag, was Crawford. He said, "I will try to help you. We might be able to get something for you. It is a slim chance, but let me make a phone call." Moments later, he discussed the dilemma with someone on the other end of the phone. Crawford finally said,

"Thanks, Dad." It had been about a ten-minute call. He then addressed the golfers. "We have to wait for his call."

A few minutes later, the call came, and the three sitting nearby leaped to their feet and approached the desk. Crawford nodded his head after lifting the receiver and said "ok" before replacing the phone in its cradle. He said, "No luck, he's trying something else."

What seemed to be an eternity as another ten minutes passed. Fifteen minutes later, another telephone call and another approaching the desk by the anxious trio. After about five minutes, Crawford lifted the receiver and gave them a Tiger Woods fist pump. He had two rooms on hold.

Crawford explained that his father oversaw the accommodations for the Elvis impersonators. They still had two rooms, but they were on different floors. There had been two cancellations. There are no connecting rooms, however. The young men would have slept in a stable if necessary. For most of the rest of that week, they were going to be rubbing elbows with Elvis of various sizes, ages, and shapes. Elvis lives.

After reloading the vehicle, Dale entered the address of their destination into the GPS, and they drove to the Beach View Club Hotel. It was about eight miles from the city of Brunswick. The hotel was located on Jekyll Island, some distance from that week's tournament's facilities. It would be a drive of about 20 miles from the resort to the golf venue. In about half an hour, they had arrived at a lovely resort. The Elvis festival was a few days away, but some tribute artists had already arrived. Black pompadours and black sideburns were prevalent throughout the hotel, atrium, hallways, coffee shop, and cocktail lounge. It appeared that Elvis had left a lasting impression long after his early demise. He had become a cottage industry.

After registering and settling into their rooms, the boys met in Dale's room to discuss Monday's plans, including a trip to the golf course. Tom suggested that he would like to use the resort's beach and other amenities in the afternoon to unwind.

Ever mindful of Frankie's whereabouts, Garney commented, "She should have no idea where we are located." Dale responded, "I wouldn't count on it. That bitch has built-in radar." Garney hoped that neither Crawford nor the Hampton Inn would divulge their new location. Perhaps she would become frustrated at being unable to locate a room and just leave. Fat chance of that happening, thought the others.

# Chapter 45: More Elvis

The tournament and their stay in Brunswick were enjoyable but routine and relatively uneventful. It was very similar to the other stops on the tour. Once again, they all cashed in on the prize money. This week, it was Garney's turn. With no sign of Frankie, he could relax, and his golf game reflected her absence. Garney placed third, winning $9600, while once again, the other two earned their entry fees. Financially, the trio was in a good position for the balance of the tour. Their results, including the three previous individual cuts, one by each, had turned in a positive cash flow. Gasoline, meals, entry fees, and accommodation were their only basic expenses. Some other golfers on the tour were already facing the financial pinch. A few of the faces disappeared, and a few new players showed up, replacing those who had slipped on golf's first rung. After three or four weeks, some entrants realized that other young golfers were capable of better golf than they could play. They were good golfers at their golf country clubs and local areas but short of the mark out here. It was a different game.

The Elvis Festival turned out to be a pleasant distraction. During the day, minibuses would gather together the various stages of Elvis. Las Vegas Elvis, black leather Elvis, and even Ed Sullivan Elvis. There were some child imitators of Elvis traveling with their beaming and proud parents. Tribute artists all. The buses drove the imitation Elvis and their guitars to the Historic Ritz Theatre and other venues. The three amigos were given tickets to the Ritz venue on the Friday night and thoroughly enjoyed the evening performances.

Garney recalls his mother telling him that her mother had said: "She was influenced towards singer Pat Boone during Elvis's heyday as the crooner was far less suggestive than Elvis." The King was pretty tame compared to the bump and grind and crotch gabbing of some of today's rock entertainers. It was the most enjoyable leg of the tour to date. One last pleasant surprise awaited them when they left the hotel after the tournament. They were advised that the Elvis Festival committee had already taken care of their bill as they checked out. They attempted to pay for their stay but were continually refused. The rooms had been paid for in full. And the hotel did not want to be paid twice.

The desk clerk was adamant when he remarked, "Don't worry about it, fellows. It will cause more problems than it's worth trying to find the right people to repay, and it is all but impossible."

# Chapter 46: The Villages

On the road again. Off to Daytona Beach for competition number five on the tour. Being in Florida brought back fond memories of Garney's trip to the Villages to visit George. It caused him to think about his home. It would be necessary to make arrangements to leave the tour at some point for a few days. He had to recharge and have a Grayling fix. He was starting to feel he had to take a break from playing competitive golf. Golf was beginning to seem that it was day after day. After all, the PGA pros on the big tour did not have a schedule with no rest or breaks between tournaments. The individual PGA pros did not enter every tournament every week. Garney and his travel mates had a conversation that evening discussing the possibility of each of them leaving the tour for some rest and recovery. Would they all take the same week, or would they take separate weeks? One of the weeks during the schedule, when they were playing in the northern leg of the tour, would be an appropriate time for a break. It was settled. They would all take the same week for their rest and recovery—a little R & R.

The tour continued through Florida, Alabama, Mississippi, and Louisiana with only two sightings or possible sightings of nemesis Frankie. Regular messages to Garney's email account professing her love were the only distraction for some time.

The events were played on well-groomed courses, and the boys continued to cover their expenses and earn some money at most of the tournaments. A point system based on wins and placings in the events was equally important to all the competitors on this tour. Those at or near the top of the mini-tour standings at the end of the season stood an excellent chance to earn entry into events in next season's Korn-Ferry tour. One step up the ladder and one step closer to the "show."

# Chapter 47: Phone Call

On a Saturday morning, they left Shreveport, which is located close to the Texas border. For the first time, none of them had made the cut for the weekend play. They decided to stay in the Shreveport region on Friday night even though none had qualified to play on the weekend. It was like having a long weekend. For the first time, they could depart before Sunday night, when the present event would be finished. The change of an extra day with no competition was needed, but it would not be anyone's desired go-to objective; they did not want to miss the cut at subsequent tournaments.

As they entered the state of Texas, Tom realized and stated there would only be three more tournaments before they would be on the northern leg of this year's tour. It would mean having a few days away from the restaurant food and the motel breakfasts. Good home cooking. A taste of home was in sight. They all needed a change from this routine of weekly travel, motels, and golf. Even with the closeness, their friendship was unwavering. They were still a good fit together as golfers and friends.

On his most recent call home to Grayling, Garney had a setback. He became almost speechless. His mother told him she had received a strange long-distance phone call from Carley Brophy. Carley had been phoned by a woman who refused to identify herself. The woman told Carley to leave Garney alone, or she would regret that she ever knew him. Maggie asked Garney if he knew what it was

152

about and if he had seen or heard from Carley while on the tour. She reminded Garney that she thought the Brophys had moved to the Carolinas.

Garney could only respond in a stammer, "I haven't got a clue." The young man was confident that Frankie was evil and deranged, trying to make his life pure hell. People were going to find out about his affair. This can't go any further! What had he done to drive her to this whacko behavior? He certainly had never encouraged her—quite the opposite.

The boys would be playing two events in Texas. It was a three-and-a-half-hour drive to the Fort Worth area for the first of the two Lone Star State venues. It was a distance of about two hundred and twenty miles. They would be able to arrive on Saturday, and Tom had called the hotel in advance to add another night to their stay in their rooms. Fort Worth was just west of Dallas and was part of an area that also included Arlington. This would be the largest populated area where an event was held during their mini-tour.

This would also be the first Sunday with nothing on the schedule. Tom had heard about the region's helicopter excursions while Garney and Dale chose to vegetate around the hotel facilities.

The boys arrived about two o'clock on Saturday afternoon and settled into their rooms at a Radisson Country Inn and Suites. The red light on the phone in one of their rooms was flashing, indicating that there was a message from the front desk. All three hoped it wasn't some bad news from their home for one of them.

Tom picked up the phone and talked to someone at the front desk. He responded, "Thank you, I'll give him the message," and then he replaced the receiver.

"Garney, it was her. Frankie left a message to say she would either drop by the hotel since you arrived early or look for you at the golf club."

Garney was crestfallen since some time had passed since her last invasion of his privacy and her last appearance in his life. He had started to believe that she had moved on. He thought that his life could return to some degree of normalcy. She seemed to be following him, and she knew his every movement. How did she do it?

# Chapter 48: Connie Francis Meets Bo

Connie Francis. Her life began normally enough. She was born to a very well-to-do family. Her father was a high-powered figure. A big name in the pharmaceutical industry. His name was associated with several generic and well-known brand medical products. Her mother was a socialite on several fund-raising boards. They were philanthropists and community leaders. Suppose that type of background can be considered normal to a young child. She spent most of her time with her nanny during her formative years. Corrine had imprinted with her mother before Nadia, the nanny, became her caregiver. Connie's mom was her only love. She didn't really know her father. Her first name wasn't Frankie, after all. She became known as Connie by all who knew her in her youth. Part of her name was true. She had been baptized Corrine Francis. She adopted the name Frankie as a form of her surname. At the age of seven, the first of many upheavals began. This is the first of several formative disturbances in her life. Her father had found another woman, and he won the custody of Connie in a bitter divorce battle. Her first stepmother was much younger than her birth mother, and she had other far more important items on her agenda than caring for a young child. Tennis and social events left little time to care for the child she had inherited with her marriage. Connie spent the early part of her education in prestigious boarding schools. There were several schools, as suspensions and expulsions were numerous. It was the first real sign of the problems. Connie longed for the attention of her birth mother, who was denied custody due to her messy affairs leading to the divorce. The young girl had been unable to spend time with her mother, who now lived at a great distance away in New Zealand. It seems both her parents were guilty of the same transgressions. Money talks!

At seventeen, a second stepmother appeared on the scene, and she was no better at caring for the young girl. She was worse. The last thing "new mom" wanted on her plate was an out-of-control, substance-abusing, spoiled teenager. Her only forte seemed to be that she was younger than wife number two, and her substantial figure was still intact. A pattern seemed to be developing. Barrels and barrels of $$ Benjamin Franklins $$ appeared to be an attraction. It did not help that her father always seemed to side with his out-of-control daughter. Fortunately, their mansion was large enough that the two females rarely had to interact with each other. They appeared to have their own separate wings. Stepmom number two spent most of her days in the lounge of their prestigious Tennis, Golf, and Country club. More boarding schools followed, and more school suspensions. Sessions with professionals, including psychiatrists. Her father even considered tough love, threatening removal from the house with no more allowance. Her allowance, which at the time was extravagant, would have been a tremendous loss to her. She had received rewards before, like a Corvette convertible, which, within three months, she had managed to crash and destroy. Fortunately, she had suffered no severe injuries. As a punishment, Dad gave her a yellow Volkswagen so that she would be more visible to the other drivers. The new car would also help her to reduce her speed. Mother number three never even left the yacht club lounge when she was apprised of the accident with the new Corvette. When she heard, she never even bothered to phone her new husband with the news. She ordered another of her afternoon gin and tonics. Now, that is tough love or really no love at all.

Connie had grown into an attractive young woman with no shortage of male pursuers. Looks and gobs of money were a valued combination among her young male suitors. Marrying that kind of money was a valued vocation by certain young men. She did not want what was available. The low-hanging fruit was not desirable. She wanted what she couldn't have.

Connie had been pursuing young golfers on the mini-tour for about three years. Some of these athletes were younger than Connie. Most of the golfers recognized her goals and her hidden motives. Unfortunately, the talented golfers advanced to the Korn Ferry tour the next season, and Connie had to start anew. On the tour, she was called 'Frank the skank.'

Frankie's obsession started in the North Carolina State's restaurant. Garney's looks immediately struck Frankie; later, she recognized Garney's ability at the golf course. This could be the train to catch to her destination.

Using her credit card, which had no limit on her spending, enabled her to pursue her prey with little concern about the expenses. Her father did not mind the arrangement. Her credit card records came to his business, allowing the office to monitor her travels. It allowed her father to see if she was attending the scheduled sessions with her psychiatrist. More often than not, she rarely participated in any of these sessions. She was usually out of control, and street drugs were not the answer. He would have been mortified if he had known how promiscuous Connie had become. She was a borderline nymphomaniac. Like father-like daughter.

Corinne Francis was psychotic; she had been diagnosed as a paranoid schizophrenic by two psychiatrists. Her reality was as she saw life. In her world, Connie was sure that Garney loved her. He just needed a little more time. Her fixation on the young golfer in the upcoming season was more substantial than it had been in her past crushes.

# Chapter 49: The Texas Tour

During the first couple of months, Connie had monitored the mini tour's path closely on the internet and stayed up to date on what was transpiring. Only twice did she travel to see some of this year's play at a golf course. On two occasions, Frankie felt that one of the amigos had spotted and recognized her. Her disguises were well done, so she was not overly concerned. The stalker limited herself to creating uncomfortable situations for Garney and his golf-playing mates. Canceling their reservations had only worked once and not all that well. The amigos had contacted their hotels ahead of time and warned them of someone trying to cancel their rooms. They explained it was a hoax. Hotel reservations had given the young golfers a secret code word to use if it was they who wanted to cancel.

Her most devious plan included a flight to Michigan. It was to discover more about the young man who was consuming her thoughts. Frankie spent several days in and around Grayling, feeling and tasting its atmosphere. She tried not to be too apparent as her master plans were yet to come. She tried to appear as if she were a tourist. It was not her first trip to the Foster's hometown. Once again, Frankie drove past the Foster home and their business. She traveled past Garney's high school and even ate lunch at the Birch Run Golf Club late one afternoon. She quickly departed the restaurant when she observed Maggie and three golfing friends leaving the 18th green after completing a round of golf. The ladies were probably coming into the lounge for a drink or lunch. Frankie exited through the pro shop, hoping to get a glimpse of George Trent. No such luck. He was probably in his office or off attending to something pertaining to the golf course's condition. Frankie was unaware that George had been watching her secretly from a table at some distance in the restaurant. George had an uncomfortable feeling about this young stranger. She had been around before asking the restaurant staff about Garney. "Was this where Garney worked?" Why was she leaving in such a rush? The woman had just started her sandwich and had not touched her fries. The drink sat untouched. Frankie had left money on the table and exited quickly through the pro shop. George greeted the ladies and asked Maggie if she knew the young lady walking toward the parking lot and her vehicle.

Maggie replied, "I don't think so. Why?" They could not make Frankie out very clearly as she walked away from the lounge. Maggie said, "She seems pretty."

George said, "Not important; I thought you knew her." He had a very ominous feeling about this young lady—call it male intuition. The professional golfer hoped she would not become a permanent resident of Grayling. Something did not seem right about her demeanor and presence.

Frankie was heading her way to Ypsilanti to register at Eastern Michigan University. She was going to audit some university courses. Some of Bob Foster's courses. She wanted to meet Bo. It was another step in the plan. Later that day, she checked out of her motel unit in Grayling. She aimed her rental car and headed south on Interstate I-75. More information had been gathered and placed in the 'Garney Foster' folder. There would still be time to email Garney later that night. How she missed him; it had seemed like an eternity. She hoped he missed her.

Frankie, who knew Bo's timetable in advance, entered the registrar's office at Eastern Michigan the following day. She paid the tuition fee to audit three of Bob Foster's classes. There was an inherent risk; Frankie knew that Bo lacked interest in academics. His attendance in class might be spotty at best. However, Bo had looked at this as a third chance opportunity. He had stated to his friends that "I ain't gonna fuck this up." His attendance and effort were miles ahead of the old Bo. Classes for Bo were like clockwork. He even considered a possible walk-on tryout the next spring with the football team. Bo's knee felt much better. His grades were oddly very respectable.

Frankie had checked into a motel. No need for a long-term commitment to a student residence was required. Long enough to meet Bo and lay some of her groundwork. She knew she wouldn't be able to get Garney yet.

The next day, the plan was in motion. The young lady received directions to the math building and the location of the lecture room. Frankie had looked up Bo's picture online in his high school yearbook. She could identify him, even though the picture was now a few years old. Locating a parking lot that was a student lot and a fifteen-minute walk to the new class followed. Garney's stalker entered the room, and his brother Bo was nowhere in sight. She exited and waited in the hallway for the straggler students to arrive at the classroom. Finally, a student was walking toward the hall entrance that appeared to be Bo. He nodded hello and entered the lecture room, which was built in an amphitheater style. It was a large class, but there were still ample empty seats. Bo waved to a male colleague, descended the stairs, and entered a row to sit with his friend. Not to be foiled, Frankie followed and sat in the seat directly behind Bo. The class began, and the young lady did not have the foggiest idea of what the math instructor was explaining.

A large screen showed figures and symbols that looked like hieroglyphics. She had seen similar scribblings as a young girl when traveling with her father somewhere in North Africa. She didn't care. Frankie planned to learn more about Garney by getting close to his brother. Real close would be okay as he had also inherited the family's good looks.

During a lull in the lecture, Frankie, now assuming the identity of one of her past schoolmates, Madison, just called me Maddy, tapped Bo on the shoulder, asking if he had a spare pen. Bo provided a Bic pen from his notebook and said, "It's okay. You can keep it." Frankie had no idea the irony of her assuming the new moniker Maddy and how appropriate it was. It suited her well.

162

Following the lecture while outside in the hall, Maddy struck up a conversation with Bo and his friend. He was oblivious that this move was orchestrated, but he was very taken by a pretty girl. Maddy suggested that they go for a coffee. Bo's friend could sense he was starting to become the fifth wheel. He had a paper to work on for next week, so he wisely begged off. The young man gave his friend Bo a quick wink and departed.

During coffee, Bo and Maddy discussed their backgrounds and which courses they were enrolled in. Everything Bo said was true, and everything Maddy said was untrue. All she could think about was how well her plan was going with her deception. It would likely take a short period of time before they became an item. She was only restricted by the schedule of the mini tour and a visit to Grayling with Bo. It depended on Garney coming home to charge his battery. Maddy had followed the tour for three years. She knew enough about the events that most of the golfers, who had accumulated sufficient points to advance to the Korn Ferry tour, took some time off in the northern section of the tour. The tournament stop in Tennessee was the closest Garney would be to home during that golf season.

Bo and Maddy met in classes, began to meet for coffee, and soon began dating. Bo became curious as to why she never made any lecture notes. She never seemed to be working on assignments. Maddy had never revealed to Bo that she was auditing his courses. Maddy didn't seem to be concerned about a grade. He wondered why she lived in a motel, which would be far more expensive than a residence. It seemed odd that Bo, of all people, would be concerned about someone else's grades. But the sex was good. The motel, all of a sudden, had become an excellent idea. He thought he might even be falling for her. Inviting her home during a school break to meet his parents seemed like a good idea. Bo thought for her to travel home to West Virginia was a long trip for the reading week. Her license tags indicated that it was her home state. She had returned her rental car to the airport and was using her yellow Volkswagen again. Frankie, until now, did not want to drive her bright yellow Bug in and around the town of Grayling.

# Chapter 50: Western Events

Frankie made flight reservations while setting the groundwork for her plan to win over her newest prey, Garney. Twice, she would use the weekends to travel to the tournaments as the mini tour continued through the states— one flight to Baton Rouge and the second to Memphis. The golf itinerary had a few stops during this time frame.

The tour had been enjoying fantastic weather. There was only one exception and one disappointment: a storm canceled a tournament. San Antonio was the unlucky city. Unusual heavy rain downfalls and storms arrived and were forecast to last the whole week. Garney had been looking forward to visiting the historic Fort Alamo and seeing the renowned River Walk in the city.

After the tournament in Dallas-Fort Worth, the tour reversed direction due to the cancellation in San Antonio, and they headed east to their next destination. Baton Rouge, Louisiana. Garney was the only one of the three amigos to make the cut in Fort Worth. After playing on the weekend, he finished fourteenth and received his entry fee as a prize. Financially, it was a less-than-stellar week for the trio. They had stayed in two rooms over eight nights in a nice chain hotel, a helicopter trip for Tom, and a tour of the vicinity.

The group had far more outgoing expenses than income realized. However, at this point, they were still well ahead financially and could continue to travel according to their initial plans.

The scheduled stops for competition after the Dallas-Fort Worth event were San Antonio, Baton Rouge, Jackson, Mississippi, Little Rock, Memphis, and then the Nashville area in Tennessee. After the first Tennessee event, the trio arranged to separate and leave for their homes. They all wanted and needed to recharge their batteries. They had varying degrees of success, and Garney was the first to win a tournament. He finished first in Little Rock and took home the $15,000 first-place prize money.

Interstate highways and motels that all seemed similar and restaurants that provided good meals which all began to taste the same. Surprisingly, no one had a falling out with either of their travel mates. The camaraderie was still going strong. Having one's own room once every three weeks certainly helped. A fourth tour golfer had requested to join them in their travel arrangements. That would have eliminated the extra space in the vehicle and the single-room accommodation. It was difficult to say no, but their arrangement had been quite successful to this point.

# Chapter 51: Suspicious Activity

Some very suspicious activity occurred in Baton Rouge and eventually happened in Memphis. This created some additional concerns for the group. Was she back? When they departed their hotel for the practice round on Tuesday morning in Baton Rouge, they discovered a rear tire had been slashed and the van windows soaped. Was this just some vandalism by local youth, or had Frankie finally returned? Later, one of their opponents was positive that he had spotted Frankie on two occasions during that event. Her hair was a different color as if it were dyed or possibly covered with a hairpiece. The only contact Garney received was the standard emails professing her love and that they were destined to be together. In one of her emails, she almost started to sound threatening. In another message, she revealed that she knew far more about him than he knew. One email ended with a flattering statement about how pretty his mother was. His family being mentioned created a fury in him. Mom and Dad were off-bounds.

The Baton Rouge tournament was played at the Jack Nicklaus-designed Country Club of Louisiana. Tom referred to the course as "a country gentleman's course." The weather cooperated, and Dale and Garney both collected cheques at the end of the tournament. Tom loved the course but had two of his worst rounds of their tour travels. For Tom, it happened not unlike anyone who golfs. Nothing worked during the two preliminary days. Drives would not find the fairway, approach shots would not find the green, and worst of all, putts would not find the golf holes.

Late on Sunday afternoon, when they returned to the van to depart for Jackson, they found two more tires had been deflated. Someone had removed the tire's valves and allowed the air to escape. It didn't require a rocket scientist to figure out who the culprit was. They filed a police report to no avail. A delay occurred for the three golfers. The automobile club dispatched a garage truck to repair an inconvenient and unnecessary problem. While in Jackson, they would have to purchase a spare tire to replace the tire that had been slashed at the hotel in Baton Rouge. What was Frankie capable of doing? So far, it had been mischievous, maddening, and annoying. Garney understandably had a much greater reason to be worried about Frankie than either Tom or Dale. It was he whom she was targeting. The other two were potential peripheral damage.

The drive to Jackson, Mississippi, was about 175 miles, and even with a delayed late start, they were able to check in to their rooms before midnight. Once again, the red message light was flashing on the phone. Once again, there was concern about a call from home for one of them. They responded, and Dale lifted the receiver. Once again, it was a female voice. A phone message asking them to take care of themselves during their journey, you never know how safe you are or how secure the van can be. Be careful. Ominous and threatening? The message planted thoughts in their minds, and they discussed that perhaps they should examine the vehicle before starting out on every occasion. They would do an exploratory walk around the van, giving the vehicle a thorough inspection before starting.

Frankie felt she had completed her tasks for this trip, as she had placed some concern in their minds about their safety. They would eventually see things her way. They needed to accept her possible regular presence as they traveled from tournament to tournament. Garney had better be nicer to her if they wanted to be safe. She still had a surprise visit ahead with Bo to his family's home in about a month. As she was known on the tour, Frankie had another more threatening visit to the Memphis tournament in her plans. Someone might get hurt if things didn't change. She was going to stop playing nice. She had physically hurt people before and could very easily do it again. Frankie knew what she wanted and felt optimistic that Garney would also know. He just didn't know it yet. She wondered if Garney knew what it was like to lose someone close to him. She could start with a pet, a colleague, a mentor, a travel mate, or even a relative. Someone or something might have to be injured or even worse to make him aware of her love. To her, it was as plain as your hand in front of your face. She was not wired together like most other people were wired. Frankie planned to reappear in Memphis, and they could fret until that time. She was starting to lose her patience. This romance was taking longer than Frankie had anticipated it would take. More drastic measures would have to be in store. Memphis would be the actual start. Garney better damn well fall in love with her. In the meantime, it was back to Eastern Michigan and plan B. Her classmate and new boyfriend, Bo, must have wondered what happened to her, and he was an essential part of her master plan. Her story would be believable, and Bo didn't think with his mind. Most of his blood was rushing below his waist.

# Chapter 52: Vacation Arrangements

The tournaments at Jackson, Mississippi, and Little Rock, Arkansas, in terms of their golf play, were generally uneventful. Lame attempts at both sites to cancel their reserved accommodations were phoned in. The hotels had been made aware not to cancel them without the group's authority. Two annoyances were avoided, but her presence had been noted. No further damage or sabotaging of Dale's van occurred. Giving the Dodge the once-over before every trip to the hotel or the golf course was just a nuisance. All three members cashed in the prize money to greater or lesser degrees at the two tournaments. More importantly, each of them accumulated more points. They all hoped to step up to the level two Korn Ferry tour next season. Just a step away from the PGA tour if they continued to gather points during the balance of the mini-tour.

One evening, the three golfers had a conversation about how close they were to their vacation and a reprieve from the tour. It was only three weeks away. Events in Memphis and Nashville were yet to be played before they began their mini vacation. They planned to join together again after their getaway, only missing the one tournament in Knoxville. All three would fly home to their respective families for the week after the Nashville tournament.

Dale had made arrangements with two other golfers on their tour. The two would drive his van to Knoxville in exchange for one of their booked rooms at the hotel. It's a fairly decent deal for both groups. Free accommodation for the one pair and a solution for the three amigos to move Dale's vehicle and their equipment to the next venue. They would be able to leave their clubs and luggage with the van. The three amigos were assured that their clubs and luggage would be well taken care of by their new friends. The two other golfers could stay that week of competition at the amigo's expense and at no cost to them personally. The room had two double beds, so the sleeping arrangement suited their needs. Dale was able to cancel the second room in the Knoxville hotel. Dale, Tom, and Garney would fly back to Knoxville after their home visits for the week. Then, they would depart immediately for Winston Salem, North Carolina, and the next golf event. There were two tournaments after Winston Salem, which would conclude the tour. One was to be held in Statesville, and the other was to be held in the Charlotte, North Carolina, area. It will have been a long but successful season. The Korn Ferry tour was in sight for the next year for all three golfers. They had accumulated almost enough points at this stage in the previous tournaments to advance up a level of competition the following season.

# Chapter 53: Malicious Act

The drive from Little Rock to Memphis, plus a stopover for a meal at an Applebee's restaurant, seemed to pass by relatively quickly. Their Memphis motel was aware of the late arrival, and the front desk was expecting them. The arrival and check-in went smoothly. Garney felt slightly uncomfortable, as if something seemed amiss. He had a sense that things were not going to go smoothly at this stop in their travels. He had a single room for this event, and he would stay extra vigilant. She just seemed to be close by. He decided not to alarm his colleagues, and he kept his feelings to himself.

They were on the second floor and close to a large, wide-open stairwell that curved into the lobby. It was a much quicker route to the main lobby level than for them to backtrack from their room to the hotel elevators.

It was soon after arriving, and they were just settled in their rooms when the front desk phoned asking if one of them could please come down to the desk. Tom remembered something he had left in the van, so he volunteered to kill two birds with one stone. He excused himself as he left the room and quickly walked to the stairs that led down to the lobby. He only reached the first step, and something tripped him. Tom pitched forward, and he plummeted through the air down the stairs. He didn't touch the stairwell for what seemed at least ten steps, and then he landed on his left wrist and left shoulder. He bounced down the remaining steps, ending up in a prone position on the bright red carpeted floor in the lobby. He felt pain in a number of areas. The evening desk clerk who had been seated behind in the office leaped to her feet and raced across the lobby to be of assistance. As she was traversing the lobby area, she glanced up and saw something or someone out of the corner of her eye.

At about the same time this happened, two hotel guests entered the area through the front doors. They were returning from a local function that they had attended. It was quite a chaotic scene. The clerk immediately beckoned for their assistance and left to summon an ambulance. In a very short time, Tom's roommates were notified.

When Garney and Dale arrived on the scene, Tom was able to relate to everyone: "Someone or something tripped me." He was very sore all over but felt that he would be okay.

Dale stated, "It's a good thing you're a decent athlete. You could have killed yourself." Everyone at the scene told Tom to stay still and let's get it checked out. Suddenly, they could all hear an approaching ambulance.

Tom reiterated, "Damn it, something tripped me," again and again. Soon, two EMRs were by his side, and they checked his vital signs and prepared him to be transported to the local emergency center for examination. In about fifteen minutes, everything had returned to some degree of normalcy. Dale would follow the ambulance in his van to the emergency ward. He told Garney he would stay in touch with him on his cell phone.

Dale asked Garney, "Do you have your phone with you." Garney responded yes with a nod. After the ambulance departed, Garney told the clerk, "This was not an accident."

The clerk responded, "I am sure I saw something moving quickly at the top of the stairs when I was coming across the lobby to help your friend. I didn't see what, but something moved. It moved very fast. It was probably an animal or perhaps a very quick person. We have a no-pet policy, but people occasionally sneak them in the back entrance."

Garney suggested, "Would she please phone the police." As she crossed the lobby, Garney said again, "This was no accident. I believe I know why this happened."

After some time, two of Memphis's finest arrived at the hotel. They went directly to the desk and spoke to the clerk. The officers received her version of the situation. There was an obvious concern on her part for any possible legal action against the hotel. The mention of her spotting something at the top of the stairs was intentionally omitted. With the troopers arriving on the scene, she realized there could be an eventual lawsuit and wanted to guard what she offered as possible evidence. She enjoyed her new position and did not want to jeopardize her future employment.

Later, Garney gave the officers his version of what had occurred. He told them he could not provide visual evidence of the incident as he was in his room at the time. What he could offer was Tom stating continually that he had been tripped at the top of the stairwell. He also said that the clerk thought she witnessed something at the top of the stairs as she had hurried to assist his friend. Tom was adamant that he had been tripped. Garney did not offer him being stalked by his 'Frankie's theory.' There was no mention of the annoyances that Frankie had been subjecting them to over the summer tour. He did not want to sound like he was a loose cannon with a hair-brained theory.

The two police officers, Owen and Casey, discussed the situation between themselves, and the fitter-looking of the two began to climb up the stairwell to the top. He then began studying the top rung's newels on either side of the stairwell.

"Owen, you had better come up here. Somebody had a tripwire tied up here. This was intentional. Whoever it was cut the line after the person tripped, but they left the knots around the posts. That's probably what the clerk saw. Someone dashed across, cut the line at both ends and fled."

Officer Casey climbed the stairs to join his partner. He said, "Whoever it was must have been quick. They probably did it when all the attention was on the young man falling or after falling down the stairs. Owen, can you get our camera from the squad car? We need to take some pictures of these knots before we cut them off. This is a crime scene, and we need some photographs as evidence. We should take some of the lobby and stairs from different angles. We should have dispatch send a car to the hospital to talk with the injured party."

Garney now felt it was appropriate to make the police officers aware of their ongoing problems with Frankie or whoever the hell she was. Before this event, it was just vandalism and a nuisance. Now, it was turning into someone's personal injury. Garney wanted to speak with the officers again. He felt he had more to reveal. Garney was positive the tripwire specialist was his nemesis' doing. He would be able to describe her and give them any details that might be able to help. He also would report to them that he would not doubt that she was staying in this same hotel. She had all kinds of nerve. Garney felt that this was just the tip of the iceberg, more to come and perhaps worse to come as they were booked here for the rest of the week. She knew their schedule and, for some reason, their itinerary. She was appearing sporadically at various tour stops and stalking him.

During his conversation with the troopers, his cell phone rang, and he answered. He was expecting a report from Dale from the hospital. It was her! Frankie had said she was so glad it wasn't him and then quickly hung up her phone. Garney quickly relayed her message to the officers. They asked for his phone in the event the suspected perpetrator called back.

Further discussion followed with all the relevant details that Garney could recall about her actions. He related all of the details, hoping not to omit any facts to the officers. The phone rang again, and this time, Owen answered. It wasn't Frankie. Dale was phoning to report on Tom. He passed the cellular phone to Garney, and it was good news this time. Bumps and bruises, ice, painkillers, and rest. They would be back at the motel in an hour or so. Nothing broken, nothing dislocated. While he healed, he would not be able to play in this event and probably not the next one following. Maybe he would be able to join them in Winston-Salem the following tournament after the Knoxville event.

The troopers had enough information to begin an investigation and stated they would like to question some of the other golfers who might know this young lady. Garney thought to himself, "She sure as hell ain't no lady." He did offer that some of the players knew her over the past couple of years. She had been appearing during some of their tournaments. He advised them of the location of this week's event and the starting time for the practice rounds on Tuesday. Garney mentioned quite a number would be at the golf course tomorrow morning practicing their putting and hitting some shots at the driving range. The officers moved across the lobby to further question the desk clerk about guests before departing in the direction of their patrol car. They wanted to question the two guests who had assisted Tom and asked for their room numbers, names, and addresses.

Garney had found a sofa in the lobby to wait for his roommates' return. He also wanted to be available to the troopers in case they had any more questions to ask him. However, the officers departed the lobby without any further questioning of the young Michigander. He would not admit it to others, but he felt much safer in the lobby than being alone in his room. It was very late, and the check-in desk and the lobby were now vacant. Garney crossed the lobby to the front desk to talk to the desk clerk, who seemed busy with paperwork and forms. She was not up to any conversation. Feeling awkward, he turned and strolled back across the lobby, moved up the staircase, and finally returned to his room.

About an hour or so later, Tom and Dale were back in the hotel, and by using the elevator, they arrived back in their second-floor rooms. The first thing that Tom wanted to discuss was his remaining golf schedule. Tom acknowledged that this event in Memphis and the next one in Nashville were going to have to be cancellations on his part. The group had already withdrawn from the following one in Knoxville to make their visits to their families and homes. This would give him nearly four weeks to heal enough to play in the final three events on the schedule. Tom reasoned that presently, he probably had accumulated enough points to advance to the Korn Ferry tour level next year. Nonetheless, he was troubled that he could be passed by other competitors during his three-week absence. Only the top few were given playing cards for the Korn Ferry tour. He was a little uneasy that he could lose his present ranking. That being the case, he may leave for his Canadian home tomorrow. He immediately started phoning the airlines in an attempt to book a flight. Tom said, "I will be able to rejoin you two in about four weeks in Winston-Salem by flying in from Toronto." He hoped that he would be able to play the final three tournaments on the tour's schedule. The Canadian medical insurance system was also Tom's concern. He did not want to run up bills in the American medical system. Tom would fly to Toronto Pearson International, where his parents would meet him for his trip to his hometown of Bobcaygeon in Ontario. Having no luck using the phone, Tom spent some time on the internet booking flights to Toronto from Memphis and Toronto returning to Winston Salem.

It was time to talk about the elephant in the room. Garney apprised them of involving the police. He told Tom, "Yes, you were tripped, and the knots at the top of the stairs indicated someone placed a tripwire there. It doesn't take a genius to figure out who was behind this. This girl is frigging crazy. You could have been killed. She used a barely visible clear fishing line for her trip wire."

Tom said, "I knew something tripped me; she should be charged."

Garney replied, "I am truly sorry. I feel it is my fault."

"I have to miss some important golf because this dipstick is stalking you. It is not your fault. What can be done by us? It is hard to prove she is responsible, but we all know it's her. I'd like to kick her ass,' but I can't lift my leg."

This small bit of humor caused the three to have a chuckle, which was probably severely needed at that moment. Each of them was privately hoping it could be over sooner rather than later.

# Chapter 54: Tom's Injury And Departure

Frankie was quite pleased with herself; maybe she had Garney's attention now. She was safely in her room. She was registered under yet another assumed name, Madison. Frankie knew the right people to be able to purchase various identifications, driver's licenses, social security cards, and passports. She had been able to see from her hotel window the ambulance had arrived and then left. Dale and Garney were walking beside the stretcher as it left the lobby. She deduced correctly that it was Tom who was injured. "I wonder how badly." When she had hastily cut and removed the tripwire, she only glanced at the body at the bottom of the stairs.

It was important that no one noticed her. She planned to remove the knots later during the night. She had yet to make her phone call to alert the other two that she was somehow involved. She witnessed Dale leave the hotel parking lot to follow the ambulance, which meant that Garney was alone in the hotel. From her third-floor room, she was provided with a perfect view of the parking entrance to the hotel lobby, and it wasn't long before she spotted a Memphis squad car. Did someone notice her removing the fish line trap? If so, it probably would now be considered a crime.

This caused her some concerns, but the police could be handled. She had dealt with the police before. It seemed all her life, from a young age, she had been dealing with the police for one reason or another. She had even been fingerprinted once, but a top lawyer had her found not guilty in the only criminal charge she faced when she was younger. Her third mother was the victim. Assault with a deadly weapon or self-defense? Not Guilty. Now, her fingerprints were in the database.

Finally, after some time, the squad car drove away from the entrance area, and she considered causing an incident involving her beloved Garney. His room was only one floor below her room. He was alone. No, the plans for the week were complete, and she was going to remain with what she had decided and stay the course of action. If it was going to work, she had to be unwavering. Garney must pay for not understanding that they were meant to be together. The boys could be so naïve; they even fell for her "could someone come to the front desk" phone call. Frankie also knew whoever responded would use the stairs and not the elevator. Frankie was a schemer and loved planning to get her way. Don't stray from the original plan. The week was starting to unfold as she had planned. They were down to two amigos.

# Chapter 55: Police Involvement

The following day was their regular get-the-feel-of-the-city Monday. They also were scheduled to drive Tom to Memphis International Airport for his flight home. Tom was able to obtain a connecting flight from Memphis to Philadelphia to Toronto, arriving at three p.m. It was a difficult phone call home. He had to explain that he was injured and would be home for three weeks, not just one. His mother was concerned about him having a concussion and wondered if he should be flying. He assured his mother he was not concussed, just sore and bruised. To his mother's annoyance, his father wanted to know if he was bringing his golf clubs home. He thought that they might get in a round or two at a local course.

Dale and Garney said their goodbyes to Tom and advised him that they would see him in Winston in three weeks' time. Before they departed from the airport, the GPS was set for North Creek Golf Club, the host for this week's tournament. The regular procedure is Tuesday practice rounds, Wednesday Pro-am rounds, Thursday and Friday elimination rounds followed by the cuts, and the weekend positioning rounds for prizes.

They were about 9 miles from the golf course in Southaven, Mississippi, which was just on the outskirts of Memphis, Tennessee. Fifteen minutes later, they arrived and had a quick tour of the facilities. Dale looked for someone in an official capacity who could assist him in withdrawing Tom from the competition due to his injury. Local golfers are often on a substitute list, hoping for a cancellation and a possible entry into the event. Dale completed the task and found Garney at the putting green, chatting with some of the other golfers who were now part of the larger traveling family. Many of these young men were getting to know each other, and a few had been staying in the same hotel. Garney had been quizzed about Tom and his status and what had happened. Garney stated the Memphis police may have questions for some of them who might know anything about Frankie and her background. They probably wanted to know if she seemed capable of such a stupid stunt.

Sorry, but "I didn't bring you guys up; it was the police officer's idea."

Two or three of them offered to let the cops know what a pain she had been to other golfers in previous years. She had driven one young golfer off the tour with some of her stunts. He was quite talented. Another player was married and had to get a restraining order to have her leave him alone. Her lawyer claimed that the order was only good for one state, and the young man would have to get a restraining order for every state he participated in. She tried to run one player, Jim something, over with her Volkswagen, and she had just missed. Frankie stalked a golfer's wife, apparently so often that the wife had to get a restraining order in their hometown.

"We are sorry it's you this year, Garney. Be careful; she seems capable of anything. There was a story that she finally gave up on one golfer and stabbed him. He was stabbed, but it was in quite a large crowd setting, leaving a baseball game, and it couldn't be proven that it was her. She was there and near the incident, but they were not able to prove she was involved. Frankie had a rough childhood but came from gobs of money. Spoiled rotten, so we hear. Can travel better and faster than we can."

Garney added, "Well, the police are looking for her. If you see her at the course, let one of the organizers know, and they can get the police involved. I will give the marshals and authorities a heads up to contact the police if it's reported that she's around."

Another added, "Garney, I hate to say this, but we are staying at the same hotel as you guys, and I swear she is registered there as well. I saw you helping Tom out this morning while we were having breakfast. I was making a waffle in the eating area, but I am sure it was her crossing the lobby to leave the hotel just after you were gone. Did you see her yellow Volkswagen in the parking lot?"

Garney quickly said, "It never ends with her; she is starting to frighten me. When we return to the hotel, I'll check at the desk to see if any woman fitting her description is staying there."

"Be careful, Garn, she will accuse you of stalking her. She is devious," one of the golfers called out as he and Dale headed toward the parking lot. They were going to go for a late lunch. Another golfer stated after them, "Not a good idea, Garn."

"Dale, what the hell can we do? This damn game is hard enough without trying to keep her out of my mind. Try rolling a twenty-five-foot putt, blasting out of a greenside sand trap, or shaping a ball around a dog leg; all I can see is her face. The only solace I seem to have recently is frequently calling home. I don't dare tell them what this bitch is doing. Mom would wash my mouth with soap if she heard what had happened to my language. She has occasionally heard Bo slip with some colorful words but usually pretends she didn't hear what he said. Did the police talk to Tom while he was at the hospital? They were going to send a car to question him. If they can prove it was her, will he press charges or file a civil suit? He will have had expenses and potential loss of revenue plus the ambulance cost, and she is apparently as wealthy as a Rockefeller."

Dale responded, "He did talk to a trooper, and if they prove it was her, and I was him, I would lawyer up and sue her pretty little ass off."

# Chapter 56: The Snake and Garney's Plan

The two amigos returned to their hotel unit. They had canceled their second room and were stretched out for some rest in what was now the shared room of Garney and Dale. Dale's old room was now unoccupied, and this fact was unknown to Garney's adversary, Frankie. To her knowledge, this was still Dale's targeted quarters. Partway through the period of rest and recovery, they were each occupied with different interests. Dale was watching an afternoon TV game show, and Garney was examining a yardage book he had acquired that morning at the golf course. The book showed information about yardages, distances, hazards, and green complexities for all eighteen holes in the round. It also included schematic diagrams of each hole. Suddenly, they were bolted upright by a blood-curdling scream from the room next door, Dale's previous room. The scream dissipated into the hallway and seemed to get further and further away.

Dale leaped from his bed and yanked open the door. At the next room's doorway, he spotted the chambermaid's cart with all the linen and cleaning materials. Looking in the other direction down the hallway at some distance, he observed the maid who was yelling, "Donna go in, Donna go in, biggy snake with a shaky tail." With this, Garney bolted from his resting place and raced to the doorway.

Garney yelled, "What the hell, who do we call." Dale responded, "Call the front desk."

Garney called the front desk, and within five to ten minutes, a maintenance employee was in the hallway outside of the room. He was followed by his colleagues just minutes later. The municipal authorities had been summoned, and the primary responsibility of the maintenance employees was to keep the snake confined to the room. About half an hour later, two personnel members from the city arrived. Appropriately attired in boots and safety equipment, they seemed well protected. One of them carried a burlap sack and the other a long pole with what appeared to be some sort of clasp on the end. The snake, when finally sighted, was identified as a timber rattlesnake, a snake that was native to the region.

The snake handler commented when he spied it, "damn good size this one, about three and a half feet."

The other handler questioned, "How the hell would it get up here and get in a room."

The snake was aggressive, taking about half an hour to corner and bag. It was fortunate that the beds were built down to the floor, and the snake was unable to seek refuge and escape beneath the beds. As they were leaving, one of the snake handlers said the rattler weighed about ten pounds and was very lethal. The chambermaid stayed the full length of the hallway away during the process, not daring to return to her cart and her job. She insisted that they look for more snakes before she would return to her duties in the room. The men placed the bag on the floor and explained that snakes don't travel in pairs. To put the maid at ease, they did another walkthrough. The front desk then assigned a second maid to assist the shaken chambermaid with the balance of her shift.

Things started to return to comparative normalcy. Dale from Florida was a little more relaxed as poisonous snakes were more common in his region of the country. Garney, not so much, although Michigan was not unsusceptible to venomous reptiles in some pockets of the state.

Dale remarked, "All these weeks in the south and the first damn snake we see is in a hotel room, go figure."

Garney responded, "It didn't get there by itself. She is still up to her friggin' treachery. I wonder how the bitch got it in there? The poor maid could have been killed, and I am sure it was not meant for her. This must be reported to the police. Where the hell is she? I know she is staying here, and it seems she is aware of every move that we make. Every move everyone makes. She probably has a room with a view so she can watch anybody approaching the hotel. Maybe we can help ourselves, do some of our own surveillance, and report it to the police. I suspect she can see the front entrance and the comings and goings of everything and everyone. I suspect her room is a room with a view of the front of the hotel."

"We are not cops, what the fuck could we do?" questioned Dale.

"I think I have thought of a plan. There must be at least thirty to forty rooms with a view like that, looking down at the front entrance and the parking lot. Most are quite some distance from the entrance, and we have never seen her on our floor, so it is probably the third floor up to the eighth floor. The nearest rooms to the entrance would be ideal for her, totaling about ten and fifteen rooms. For her, the closer she is, the better, maybe even the third floor. We are talking about a dozen rooms."

"Right above us, right? No way," answered Dale. With his mind in full gear, Garney replied, "We don't have a front view, so no, not above us but across the hall and up at least one flight."

"So, what's the plan, Sherlock, if you believe she is in this hotel? How can we smoke her out of her den onto Baker Street?"

The Baker Street reference went over Garney's head, and he said, "Here is what I think would work. One of us, ok me, goes out the back exit and walks around where I can stay out of sight behind some cars. Where I can observe the windows for any activity. Give me time to get in place, and then you leave by the front doors. Walk to the van, and I will watch for any movement in the suspected windows."

"You actually think that might work. I guess it's worth a try. How many times will we try this? A few. I don't think she is here in this hotel anymore. I think she moved to a safer location. After all, a tripwire and rattlesnake, how do you top that? Maybe you should just marry her." Dale got his hand up quickly to grab a pillow in fast flight aimed at his head.

Garney asked, "Want to give it a try now."

"Ok, it's as good a time as any. Let's do it," said Dale as they began to put their plan in motion. Timing was important. Garney left the room and headed for the back stairwell. Dale was going to give him a ten-minute start before he departed the lobby for his van.

Garney exited the rear of the hotel and walked along the back side of the building, past the service entrance, past the garbage bin's wooden fences, and past the hotel laundry with its hot air and smell of clean sheets. Two maintenance men who had assisted with the snake problem earlier were sitting on the loading dock having a smoke. They nodded as he passed by them, and he responded with a "How are you doing?" The first part of the plan was not what he had hoped for. Garney hoped he would not be seen on his venture. As he approached the front of the hotel, his luck changed for the better. Two large white box trucks and a large van in the hotel lot protected him from any view from the building. He edged around the second large truck and had the view he had hoped for. The windows that he wanted to see were highly visible from his hiding location.

The only exception was the entire top floor, which was reflecting the lowering sunrays. Moments later, Dale exited the hotel's front door and meandered into the parking lot. There it was, precisely at one of the windows that Garney had predicted. A female was seated at the window watching Dale as he headed for his vehicle. The person then rose to her feet. He was positive it was her. Overly exuberant and excited, he left his vantage point and jumped out and fist-pumped toward Dale. Garney pointed to the window. As Dale turned to look, the drapes were being drawn rapidly. Garney did not care. He knew where she was.

Garney ran toward Dale and said, "Let's report her to the desk and have them call the police. I was right. I was right!! The exact room that I suspected. I knew she was staying here."

Dale replied, "There was a bit of luck that it was the right room. I admit it was a helluva good idea. Maybe the rest of this tour will be less stressful. I hope they have something to charge her with."

"I am positive it was Frankie; I had a real good look, and I think she stared me right in the eye. The trip wire would be a start for any charges. The snake if it can be proved somehow." The two walked quickly, and half jogged back in the direction of the hotel entrance, anxious to report their observation and theory to the property management.

Garney felt he could see an end to this continual harassment. He could almost taste it. He could begin to feel normal again.

# Chapter 57: Another Snake And Garney's Departure

The two young men entered the front doors and walked briskly across the lobby to the front desk. A young male in his issued red hotel blazer left his chair in the office and approached the two guests. He began by asking if he could be of any service. The young man's badge indicated that his name was Yesim. Garney and Dale explained to the clerk the negative situations that had occurred during their hotel stay. The clerk was aware of most of what they were describing. He knew of the fall down the stairs by a guest golfer. He continued to refer to it as a fall even though they continually corrected him, referring to the incident as an intentional trip. Dale said they knew who tripped their friend, and that person was staying in a third-floor room in this hotel. The young clerk seemed to be in quite a dilemma. His manager was out for dinner. Yesmin was now in charge, and he was a relatively new employee. It was an enigma; he had no idea what his following action or move should be.

Garney suggested or rather requested that he phone the police. This was disregarded as the clerk stated, "We should wait for the manager."

Persistence and an explanation that the police wanted to talk to this woman when she was located only had Yesim further entrench his stance. Calling the police to question a guest had his future unemployment written all over it. Finally, Garnet said they would use their cell phones to beckon the Memphis police. This seemed to be agreeable with the young clerk. Now, he could not be held directly responsible for any repercussions from the female guest or the manager. He did provide the city of Memphis police's telephone number, which was attached to the cradle of the hotel's desk phone.

Dale called and spoke to a desk sergeant who immediately transferred him to the investigation bureau. Within moments, Dale was describing the scenario to a detective whose name ironically was Friday: J Friday, John, not Joe.

Sergeant Friday listened carefully to the tripping tale and the snake saga and then stated he and his partner would see them in the lobby in about twenty minutes. He then requalified the time. He wanted to look at the file first, so it might take a little longer, "give us forty-five minutes."

Garney and Dale left Yesim and the front desk and made their way to one of the seating areas on the opposite side of the lobby. Forty-five minutes became an hour, and the two young men decided to wait for the detectives outside the hotel entrance. They would wait in the protected vehicle pull-through area, where guests would drop off and load their luggage. They were marking time for about ten minutes when Garney finally spotted an obvious unmarked police vehicle arriving in the parking lot. It was a black car with black tires, slightly black windows, mirrors, and the telltale black battering ram attached to the front bumper. Hardly unmarked.

Sergeant Friday and his colleague exited the vehicle and strode toward the entrance. Garney and Dale moved to meet them at a point between the hotel and the unmarked vehicle. Garney peered back to the third floor of the room that he had identified earlier. Nothing had changed. The drapes were still drawn.

Entering the hotel, the four men selected the seating area that Dale and Garney had used while awaiting the detective's arrival. The details of the tripping incident and the snake were explained to the police, most of which were already known by the Memphis police department. They related details of the other times Garney was stalked during the past few weeks. Prior incidents with her stalking other young golfers in previous years. These stories have been related to them by their golfing colleagues. The other officer, whose name was O'Reilly, talk about typecasting, flipped pages, and took notes. The fact that the tire slashing was reported in Baton Rouge to the Louisiana State Police was passed on to the officers. The detectives spent about another half an hour questioning the young golfers. The detectives asked them to stay where they were, and then they crossed the lobby to the front desk.

Earlier, the hotel manager had been brought up to date by his young desk clerk, Yesim. The manager had returned from his dinner about half an hour ago. He was at the desk in time to greet the detectives. The manager introduced himself as William Travis and asked how he could help. Detective O'Reilly mentioned they would like to speak to one of their guests. Manager Travis replied that two of his senior guests had been quite upset earlier when the police interviewed them. They insisted they had only assisted a young man who was hurt during an accidental fall. The couple stated that they had arrived after the fact and were not witnesses to the actual tumble. They also said that they would rather not get involved as they were from out of town.

Travis asked the police why they wanted to talk to another of his guests. "Were they involved somehow?" The hotel had a stake in this questioning. Were there any reasons why the police had to discuss this accident with another one of his guests?

At this point, Sergeant Friday spoke up and indicated that they were expecting better cooperation than they were receiving. "Two other recent crimes have been perpetrated in your building in the last year, and we can make this considerably more difficult for you. That is if that's the way you choose to play it."

Sergeant O'Reilly added, "We need to know the room number on the third floor, second window to the right of the entrance, as you are facing the building. We also need to have the name of the occupant and their home address. We would like to have it now!"

The manager asked if something like this required a search warrant. They stared at him, and after reflecting for a few seconds, he suggested, "I think I can help." It made very little sense to oppose the city's district law enforcement agency. In the past, law enforcement was very responsive when the hotel required the police.

They had been reasonably prompt when called to the property for any assistance. Upon examining the registration ledger, he was able to give the name of Madison Wertz from Columbus, Ohio, to the detectives. She was registered in room 316 for the rest of the week until next Sunday. She had checked in for her stay yesterday at about noon.

The officers asked the manager to accompany them to her room. He responded that he could call the room and indicate she needed to check with him at the desk. One of the officers stated that this was not police policy and that they would rather speak to her in her room. She seemed street-smart, and fleeing was a distinct possibility. The threesome headed for the elevator, and Friday again asked Garney and Dale to stay where they were seated and that they would talk to them again in a short while.

The officers and the manager entered the elevator, and the manager pressed the panel for the third floor, causing an upward movement with a humming sound. They slowly passed by the second floor in their transit. A gentle stop and the doors silently slid open. The manager, Travis, exited and led the party to his left. They passed by a few doorways and an ice machine alcove. He stopped at room 316 and gently knocked. There was no answer. He gently rapped again to no response.

The third time, he announced "housekeeping," only to receive no answer once again. He declared, "I don't hear anything; I don't think that anyone is in there unless they are sound asleep."

Friday stated, "You must have a passkey or a card." The manager queried, knowing the answer, "Can we enter without her permission if she is absent or even if she is in her room?" Sergeant Friday, without answering, asked, "Could you call a chambermaid to bring some fresh towels to our location."

Within a few minutes, a maid arrived with a fresh armload of towels. She was asked to announce that she had fresh towels and see if there was any response. If no one answered, then use her passkey and unlock the door. When the door was unlocked and slowly opened, it was discovered that the room was unoccupied. No guest. No luggage. No evidence of any occupancy. All that was remaining in the room, which they were able to see immediately, was a handwritten note. It was written on hotel stationery and placed on the night table with two envelopes. The note explained that one of the envelopes contained the balance of her room bill for the week through to Sunday. The other envelope held an appropriate gratuity for the chambermaid. Nothing else. Everything else was gone.

At this point, the manager thought he was aware of some noise coming from the bathroom. He slowly opened the door and then couldn't close it fast enough. Being extremely cautious, he quickly jammed some of the new towels under the door to prevent any possible exit.

Sergeant O'Reilly quickly asked him, "What the hell are you doing?" as he stepped toward the bathroom door. "Is there a body in there or something?"

"Worse, it's another big damn rattlesnake. Don't open the door! It looked like a bag or something was on the floor near the toilet."

Friday, who was not a fan of reptiles, reached under his jacket behind his back and drew out his revolver. "Don't even think of opening that door while I am here, or there is going to be bullets flying all over this fucking room. Who do you call to get it out of here?"

Manager Travis said, "They were here yesterday to take one away. I will call them now. Oh God, I hope this is not some infestation of some sort. I will leave and find another job."

Friday replied, "I think your infestation is finished. It left with Miss Wertz. I believe she was the source of your problem. It seems she was using them as weapons. Some twisted mind she seems to have."

Sergeant O'Reilly asked the manager, "Could she possibly exit through the lobby unnoticed with her luggage? Perhaps there was another exit that she could have used to leave secretly? Does the hotel have a security camera system so that forensics could take the tapes with them for examination?"

Travis explained, "People crossing the lobby with their luggage is a regular occurrence, nothing unusual. It is nothing that would set off any red flags or alarm bells. As for the security tapes, I have asked ownership for an upgrade for some time. We have tapes, but they are not of the best quality."

"What about any coverage in the halls for when she put the snake in what had been the boys' other room? We would like to dust this room for fingerprints. Do not have forensics dust before maintenance removes this snake. Just make sure forensics doesn't open that bathroom door. If there are any prints here, there should be plenty in this area. Have maintenance or the city remove this snake before forensics begins their work."

Friday offered to the manager, "Excuse us, we have to have another session with the two young golfers. We will see you about the security tapes after we have talked with them."

The small party left the room, headed for the elevator, and retraced their steps to the area near the front desk. After about a five-minute discussion with room clerk Yesmin, the two officers returned to Dale and Garney to have them further add to their statements. The manager busied himself arranging for the video department to come to the hotel and replace the videotapes. The hotel was under contract with an outside firm for their security equipment. That firm had a reputation for cutting corners with the camera equipment that it had installed in various local businesses in Memphis. Manager Travis had to be adamant for a technician to come immediately as the police required the tapes now! This was typical of this outside firm's service. You get what you pay for. This firm had tendered the lowest bid during the initial hotel construction and the video equipment installation. The company's service and its equipment were showing it.

The detectives explained to the young men that they had done some nice work, but they should leave the investigation to the authorities. This suspect appears very dangerous and could be capable of doing worse. They were pleased to have some more facts to work with, and they would try to bring her in for questioning. Before departing, the officers explained that she had left the hotel, probably by the side or back entrance. " A second snake was found in the young lady's room, so be cautious."

Dale offered the officers another description and added that sometimes she had been seen driving a yellow Volkswagen Beetle. In some of the cities where she had been observed, the stalker was driving a yellow 'bug.' Sergeant Friday asked if either of the boys had possibly noticed the plate number. Garney could only state that he thought it was a West Virginia or Ohio tag. With the conversation concluded, the detectives exited the hotel to return to their police station.

The boys returned upstairs to their room. When Garney opened the door, he noticed an envelope taped to the television screen. Upon opening the envelope, he removed a handwritten note written on hotel stationery. It stated, "WELL YOU WON THIS LITTLE SKIRMISH BUT I WILL WIN YOU OVER YET. YOU WILL BE MINE" LOVE FRANKIE. SEE YOU SOON.

Dale said, "This is some more evidence that we must report to the police. How the hell does she get into these rooms? We know she has been able to enter these rooms illegally.

Garney replied, "I am going to turn this in to the front check-in desk as more evidence for the detectives. I am going to ask how she gets into all these damn rooms. I would like to know how she does it. The hotel industry must have an idea of what she uses to enter rooms. In the meantime, I'll have them deal with the police about this note."

When Garney arrived at the desk, he turned in Frankie's note and asked an elderly clerk to please get in touch with the police. The desk clerks seemed to be ever-changing. Garney explained it was an ongoing investigation and that this was more evidence.

Garney asked the older woman, "Is there any way a criminal could enter a room without a key?" She replied probably not; their system was built to prevent such an occurrence, but sometimes it was intermittent. Garney thought to himself, "That's a lie. I know damn well firsthand it doesn't work most of the time and probably fails all of the time."

Garney returned to the room, and Dale showed him what he had found online while he was gone. It explained what criminals were capable of doing. Simple to more complex devices were used by dishonest people to enter areas not designed to be entered by them. This only caused more reasons for Garney to be concerned. Where was he safe? Was his family safe? Should he give them a heads-up for their potential safety? He opted to give it a little more time. His family knew nothing of his troubles, and certainly, Maggie would have asked him to return home to Grayling immediately.

The following day, aside from this activity, more peripheral damage occurred. One of the hotel chambermaids quit her job when she heard about the second snake. She would not stay and work in what she believed to be a snake-infested viper pit.

# Chapter 58: Break And Enter And Vamoose

Frankie was used to changing her plans on the move. One thing that this young lady had was the ability to adapt. She was now a suspect in a crime, and she was sure that she would be wanted for questioning. The authorities would not take lightly to her bringing poisonous reptiles into a hotel. The tripwire would be hard to prove, but the police might have a circumstantial case. In the meantime, Frankie had observed, from her vantage point, the comings and goings of the guests at the hotel. She wanted to be able to notice the arrival of a police car. She had a feeling that she had probably been spotted. Frankie was certain Garney had seen her in her hotel room window. It was nearly time to exit stage left.

Frankie always thought and planned ahead. In the event that the police were contacted, she would be prepared to leave at a moment's notice. As was her custom, she had previously checked the available exits when and if such a situation occurred. She had found a side exit that was closest to her rental vehicle to use for a quick departure. Her only concern was the second timber rattlesnake. It was in a burlap sack tied at the top and placed in the bathtub. What if a chambermaid were to enter the room first? The snake could cause some delay, which would help in assisting her quick flight from the hotel. If she were to require an immediate departure, her luggage would have been packed. A small suitcase, which she used for situations like this, was packed, ready, and placed on the bed. Money in envelopes with an explanation, check. She did not need the police to be searching for someone who had skipped out on their hotel bill to be included in her other crimes and indiscretions. Frankie was concerned that she was making mistakes for the first time. It started with the first snake; perhaps it was placed in the wrong room. It had been intended for Dale's room. She was concerned that it was Garney's room where she had released the reptile.

Oh-oh, there it was, an unmarked car was turning into the hotel parking lot from the adjacent street. Time to bail. Frankie quickly entered the bathroom and gingerly removed the burlap sack from the bathtub. She placed the bag on the floor and promptly untied the drawstring, and as fast as she was able to, she exited her bathroom. This would possibly buy her some time if she required it. She closed the bathroom door behind her as swiftly as possible. Everything was in place. Frankie grabbed her small suitcase, stepped into the hall, and quietly closed her room door behind her. It was mere moments before she was moving down the stairs to the rear exit. She moved quickly and cautiously out to her vehicle.

As she entered her vehicle, she eyed the two officers shaking hands with Garney and his friend Dale. The group was at the far side of the hotel parking lot close to the main entrance, and it was too far for them to be able to recognize that it was her driving towards the street.

First things first, she had purchased the snakes from an old-timer in the countryside at a rural homestead. It was about twenty miles out of town. No questions were asked, and no answers were given—only an exchange of snakes and money. The old-timer had some concern for her safety. He continually ensured that she knew how to handle the sacks and their contents very carefully. Later that afternoon, he had heard about a snake in a hotel on a local radio station and immediately knew it was probably one of his. He wasn't sure what she was up to, but his intuition told him it was not any good. She had given him some cock and bull story about lab work and milking the snakes to produce an anti-venom.

Frankie now considered perhaps buying a couple more snakes. One would fit nicely into a golf bag. One thing this psycho was She was disciplined and rejected that thought immediately. This was not on her itinerary for this trip. Her plans did not include getting sidetracked. This was a crossroads on this trip. Her plans had included being here for the week.

She might book into another hotel. It was a little risky, as other golfers on the tour were scattered in hotels around the city. She, in all likelihood, would be recognized by one of them. Memphis was no longer a safe place for her, especially as a possible fugitive who could probably be identified.

Bo would be wondering where the hell she was. Where had she gone? This was the second time that there was no Maddy to be found. Not in classes, not at the motel, nowhere was he able to locate her. He was getting to enjoy and expect the benefits of her companionship.

Frankie or Madison thought a quick return to Ypsilanti was her best plan of attack. The last thing she wanted to do was foul up her plans for the trip to Grayling with Bo. Madison needed to maintain her relationship with Bo. A reunion with Garney was the end goal. What would Bo's reaction be? He would just have to live with it. He would probably understand. He seemed to be the type to not fret for very long. She set the rental automobile's GPS for the local airport. This was followed by a flight to Detroit, where she picked up her Volkswagen and returned to Eastern Michigan's campus. This venture to Memphis hadn't been a total failure. It was less than the success that she had hoped for. On the plus side, fear was intensified in her quarry. Fear enough to help Garney see her side of their relationship and realize he truly was meant to be with her.

Six hours after leaving her hotel in Memphis, Madison was unlocking the door to her motel room in Ypsilanti. She would be able to see Garney in about two weeks. Frankie had continually checked the entries and withdrawals from the tour on the internet. She was aware that Garney would be returning to Grayling in two weeks. All she could think of now was having to go to these three damn classes. Twice a week for three more weeks. Six more classes and probably four or five rolls in the hay a week with Bo. He was so rough around the edges when compared to Garney. Madison wondered what genetic traits and behaviors older brother Steve possessed. She was sure that a second brother-in-law like Bo would not be to her liking. In her view, these dumb jocks were all the same. Madison did not believe that Garney could possibly fall into that category. Golf was different. Garney and Bo almost seemed like two brothers from different mothers. You knew they were related, but they were different, oh so very different.

She was aware that the three amigos would be taking a break from the tour after the Nashville event. They had withdrawn from the tournament in Knoxville. Fortunately, that had coincided with a reading week at most universities. It was a great stroke of fortune. She couldn't have prepared it any better when she was planning this reunion. They would all be in Grayling together for that particular week. She wondered if Steve would be home from Bowling Green, perhaps with his fiancée—one big happy family meeting for the first time. Connie, Frankie, or Madison was sinking deeper into her own fantasy world. Her imagination had hit a speed bump, and there was no way for her to return to the straight road. She was at the point of no return. This was a path to tragedy for someone unless she were to come to her senses. Her entire plot was preposterous and almost laughable. Money was no object, and she needed professional help. Unfortunately, her formative years gave her limited stability, no foundation, and no direction. For her father, it was far easier to meet her wants and needs than to provide what was really needed: a supportive, understanding family. Connie understandably had gone amok. To this day, her father bought for himself what seemed to be some semblance of peace by providing her with all the material wants that she desired.

To this point. It wasn't easy to understand how Frankie was obtaining her information about the tour schedule, the tee times, where the golfers were staying, and when they entered or withdrew from events. She seemed to have the resources to let her know everything necessary about the tour schedule. Her computer skills allowed her to hack the tour's computers and locate entries, player contacts, and where they were staying during each tournament. She was able to move in and out of the committee's computers at will and to obtain what she required for her plans.

In very short order, Bo was at her motel room door. Though he would not admit it, he missed her and passed by the motel regularly. When he was passing her residence this time, he spotted her yellow Volkswagen. For the first time, the sex wasn't the only part of the package. He was actually quite fond of her.

When Madison opened her door, he was happy and angry at the same time. He was so glad to see her and wanted to know where the hell she had been. Why had she left without telling him what she was doing or where she was going? He felt he deserved better. The shoe was on the other foot as he received the treatment that he usually gave to women. He was not accustomed to playing second fiddle.

The two went for dinner at a Roadhouse restaurant and discussed what they had been doing. Bo had little to offer and explained to her what had occurred in classes while she was gone. Madison feigned interest, and you could see signs of boredom in her expressionless face. It did not interest her in the least. She nodded enough to maintain Bo's interest. The trip to Graying was critical. Madison concocted a believable story, and Bo had no reason to believe it was another fabrication of her activities and her past. After dinner, they returned to the motel for the night.

# Chapter 59: Contacting Tom

The tournament in Memphis concluded without any further dramatics, and both Dale and Garney made the cut-off for the weekend play. As the week progressed, the duo missed their friend, Tom. It seemed empty without his pleasant nature and carefree Canadian one-liners. On Sunday, both players played very good golf rounds to move into a position to recover their entry fees. It was not a big payday, but the golf expenses were being covered along with their accommodation, food, and travel costs. They had recovered the cost of their entry fees into the tournament. Dale assumed correctly that Frankie had left the area as no further incidents had occurred. However, this failed to prevent Garney, in particular, from being constantly alert to his surroundings during the week. He would anticipate her presence with every movement on every golf hole and every yellow car they passed.

Upon completing the distribution of the Memphis committee's tournament prize money, the two amigos loaded their golf equipment into the Caravan and began their journey to Nashville. This would be the last stop before departing for their home areas and a break away from the tour. It was arranged that they would meet up with Tom in Winston-Salem upon their return from their mini vacations.

They had stayed in contact during his absence with frequent telephone calls. Tom wanted to be updated on the tournament results and how his two amigos were doing. They seemed to be in contact more with Tom than their own families. He was having a speedy recovery from his fall as he was following his physician's instructions carefully. During one phone call, Tom indicated that he had taken several practice swings in his parents' backyard. Later, arrangements would be finalized as to what flights each would be traveling on so that they would be able to reconnect.

It would be the third last stop on the tour. They agreed to stay in touch during the next two weeks to complete their plans. If it were only so simple? It might be the final time that Garney would ever see either of his two new best friends. The trip ran smoothly, and they arrived in Nashville that evening. As per their regular routine, the two traveled to the next venue on the Sunday after a tournament had been completed. Many other competitors still opted to remain in the area where they had just competed. After a good night's rest, the other competitors would travel to the next event on Monday.

# Chapter 60: The Trip Home

Everything was normal, except that someone had tried to cancel the reservations for their stay at the Drury Hotel in Nashville. As their request not to accept any cancellations, their room awaited them. Frankie's plans had again been thwarted, more a nuisance and inconvenience to the hotel management than it was to the golfers.

Re-examining their schedule that evening reminded them that this week's tournament would be played at Halton Hills Golf Club. By using the map system in Dale's laptop computer, it could be located very easily. The next day, on their tour of Nashville, they would travel to the golf club and do a quick check of the golf course. Garney was struck by all there was to see and do in the country music capital. He did favor country music. Knowing the answer in advance, he wondered if they could beg off the pro-am, giving them another day to tour the city. On Tuesday, again, a practice round would allow them to play and familiarize themselves with the golf course.

The following day, on Wednesday, they played in the pro-am. It was enjoyable and unremarkable. Once again, the amateur members were very pleasant people. One of the parties in Dale's foursome continually remarked, "He couldn't get over all the young professionals' abilities." He stated, "I was at the driving range warming up, and you guys were bombing them out there."

On Thursday, the first eighteen holes would begin with Dale and Garney being drawn to play in the same threesome, and being together brought out their best game for both of them. At the end of that first day, they were in fifth and sixth place, only three shots from the leader. Garney was fifth, and Dale a stroke behind in sixth.

The following day, on Friday, their continued good play kept them near the top of the leaderboard. They had easily made the cutoff and would again be around for golf on the weekend.

Late Sunday afternoon, with only a few holes to play, in separate groups, each knew they were in or near the lead. Unlike the PGA, large leaderboards were not placed around the facility, which allowed the players to have a view of their position during the play. When the event was concluded, they had finished second and third, both missing makeable putts on the last few holes. Garney was two strokes behind the winner, and Dale finished three back—a decent payday followed for both players. More importantly, the points accumulated in the tournament put the two friends in an excellent position to receive their card for next year's Korn Ferry tour. During the season, the top Korn Ferry players occasionally were given a spot to play in one of the PGA tour events.

After returning to their hotel, organizing and fine-tuning were completed for their respective trips to Tampa and Detroit. Both had been able to book flights for the following morning. Their parents had agreed to meet them at the airports nearest their homes. The four parents and Wedgy would be excited to see their sons and his master.

Dale contacted the golfers who were borrowing his van and taking their luggage and golf clubs to the next event. Garney contacted the hotel in Knoxville to alert them of the name changes in the room, cancel the second room, and book accommodations for the three amigos the following Sunday. All three friends agreed to a change of plans. They would meet in Knoxville and leave together for Winston-Salem for one of the last tournaments of the year.

On Monday morning, Dale and Ganey drove to the other golfers' hotel to pick them up. The other golfers loaded their clubs and luggage into the vehicle, and the group headed for Nashville airport. Garney and Dale wished them well at the next event and stated they would see them the following Sunday in Knoxville.

Dale was the fortunate one of the two as his direct flight departed at 11:35 a.m. while Garney's departure for Detroit was at 2:10 in the afternoon with a connecting flight in Washington, DC. Several hours later, Garney's flight was descending into Detroit's Metropolitan Airport, almost home. Darkness had descended as the plane disembarked its passengers—a long day with a lengthy drive ahead to Grayling and his bed.

Going to the baggage claim area was unnecessary, as he had just a small backpack carry-on. Within moments, he saw his mother and father and huge embraces followed by a few tears from Maggie. Even though it was difficult, Stephen and Garney held back their tears because men are not supposed to show their emotions.

The conversation between Garney and Maggie started and then continued all the way back to their vehicle. Before asking about his brothers, Garney wanted to know how Wedgy was doing. His cat was now getting on in years. Before asking about his brothers, he wanted to know if they had seen Mr. Trent and how he was doing. "Was the golf course in good shape?" An abundance of questions that had answers he hardly heard. His mother did mention that his brother Bob would be home for the week. It was reading week at college, and he was bringing a friend home with him to visit and meet his parents. It finally clicked with Garney that his mother had mentioned Bo and a friend.

"Is it a girl or a guy?" Garney asked.

"It's a young lady called Madison. Bob thinks she is very nice, so don't tease him."

"What about Steve? Will he be here? I think we are running out of bedrooms, and I have been looking forward to sleeping in my own bed. I don't particularly want to share a bedroom with a brother."

"You don't have to worry. Steve is not coming home. He has some internship work that he must do. Madison can use Steve's old room."

"Have you met her yet, Mom? Has she been up here before?"

Maggie replied, "We only know what Bob has told us, and other than they have been seeing each other for a while, we know very little. They will be here tomorrow afternoon."

At long last, the Foster household was just ahead on the right, home at last, a week of forgetting everything negative. Being able to tell his parents what it was like on the tour. Seeing Wedgy, visiting George. A week of relaxation. Wedgy was at the door when he entered the house—a happy reunion between the young man and his pet. The two old friends were enjoying each other's company.

Garney spent the rest of the evening talking with his parents, telling them what he dared. It was late, and he was tired from the trip home. The family called it a night. Tomorrow will be an interesting day. Disruption and chaos. Anger and violence.

# Chapter 61: George

The Foster family arose happily, unthinkingly, facing a new day the next morning. Maggie was delighted to have her one son home and another son arriving in the afternoon. Stephen had arranged for his assistant manager to open the hardware store, and he was going to spend the day at home. He was anxious to meet Bo's lady friend. Bo seemed a little more serious with this latest friend, more serious than others he had dated. Maggie prepared a delicious breakfast of eggs and home fries. Stephen pitched in and fried the bacon while Garney toasted the bread. It was like old times on a Sunday morning ten years ago. No worries. Wedge was never more than two or three steps away from her master from the time he had arrived. When Garney saw Wedge on arrival the previous evening, she appeared to have gained a good amount of weight and then lost it all the following day. Maggie suggested that Wedge's hair was standing on end because the cat was so excited at seeing her master, which gave her a much larger appearance.

Eleven a.m. arrived very quickly that morning, and Garney asked if he could drive to the golf club to see Mr. Trent. Stephen stated, "Remember, Bo will arrive home early in the afternoon. It would be nice if you were here to greet him. Don't be too long; you have all week to visit George." Garney kissed his mom goodbye and headed for their suburban vehicle. "I won't be very long, see you soon." Wedge was right on his tail. Garney added to no one in particular, "I'm going to take Wedge with me."

Wedge curled up on the seat next to his master as they wound their way to the country club. Garney hoped that Mr. Trent would be at the club, although it was a Sunday. He thought that he should have called first, but Garney had hoped to surprise his mentor. The young man parked the vehicle and told Wedge that he wouldn't be long. Closing the car door, he walked from the parking lot in the direction of the pro shop. As he entered, George from behind the counter spotted him.

"Well, look what the cat dragged in. How's my favorite young golfer? boomed George. "Did they run you off the tour, or did you run out of money? I know it's not the money, as we have been following your exploits, and your pockets are getting full by now. You are making everyone around here proud. See, you have won one tournament."

Garney blushed and proudly stated, "My point total was pretty good, and it was nearing enough to move up to the Korn Ferry next season."

An hour passed, and Garney knew that he had to leave. In the interim, he told Mr. Trent about some of the events, his mates he traveled with, and how the golf was terrific. Never once did he refer to Frankie—there was no need to upset others. The way the three handled their expenses impressed George. The two hotel rooms being rotated made good sense. A little privacy once every three weeks was ideal and probably much needed.

After he visited the golf club, Garney began to leave for his home, wishing Mr. Trent to have a good day. Wedge awoke from his sleep as he re-entered the car, relieved that his master had not left him again. He also reminded George that he would drop by again before he returned to the tour. Garney began the drive home down the laneway he had used many times before. The young man felt carefree as he was in such familiar surroundings. He looked forward to seeing Bo and his new lady friend.

# Chapter 62: Bo, Madison And Garney

It was daybreak in Ypsilanti, and Madison had been awake for hours. Her nerves were creating an almost panicked feeling. How would this work out? In her mind, Bo would understand, and Garney would be so impressed that she went to this trouble and this length to be with him.

Bo was still sleeping like a baby. It was almost like he had no conscience, not a worry in the world. Finally, Madison decided to rouse Bo as it was nearly eight o'clock. She felt that after a good breakfast and the drive to Grayling, they might be getting a little tight on time for their scheduled arrival. Madison also needed to be doing something, anything, as she was starting to feel the pressure of what was ahead. She was sure that Bo's parents would welcome her and completely understand why she had done what she had done. Bo would move on as if everything had worked out for the best. Garney would now understand how much he meant to her. He would realize he was foolish to have rejected her these last few months. He could have saved a lot of trouble and discomfort if they had been able to have a relationship from the first time they had met.

Maddy and Bo, now roommates, showered and prepared to leave for the drive north. Small suitcases were placed in the Volkswagen's boot for the few days' stay. Madison had checked last evening to ensure the West Virginia plates were mounted on her car.

She had changed them so often that she wasn't sure if she was from Ohio or some other state.

Madison asked Bo what Graying was like. "Was it a small town or a medium-sized town? Did they live right in town or outside of the town? What did his father do for a living?"

She knew the answers to all of her questions but felt it helped to keep up her ruse for as long as possible. Bo had never offered this information in the past, and he was pleased to pass information on his background to Madison. He hoped she would be able to understand his parents and his family background better. This was new territory for Bo as he usually kept things like that to himself. He never considered it interesting or anyone else's business. The drive moved smoothly, with only a short stop to refill the gasoline tank at a service center and to grab a sandwich to go.

Grayling and the Foster home were approaching, and Madison was becoming more apprehensive. This was the most significant conundrum she had ever engineered or been involved with. As Bo turned the wheel to enter the family driveway, Madison temporarily lost her nerve. She blurted out, "Let's take a spin downtown first so that I can gather myself. I am a little nervous."

Bo said, "Okay, but we can't delay this much longer. Just relax, my parents are terrific people. Okay, one quick drive down the main street."

Maggie was at the kitchen window and saw the yellow vehicle start to enter and then quickly leave. "I thought they were here, Stephen, false alarm."

After about twenty minutes this time, the Volkswagen turned in and headed for one of the home's parking spots. The two exited the vehicle, and Bo removed the overnight bags from the front trunk of the Volkswagen. As they walked to the door, Maggie moved to open the door to greet them. Madison was charming as she was introduced to Bo's parents. This personable young lady immediately enamored Maggie. How fortunate Bo was to have found such a nice girl. The four moved to the family room, and Maggie offered some tea or coffee, which was politely declined by all.

Maggie asked Madison, "Have you and Bob eaten lunch?"

Bo replied, "Not yet, Mom. In a little while, we had a sandwich on the way."

The initial introductory conversation was barely fifteen minutes old when Stephen mentioned he thought he heard Garney driving up the driveway. When he first turned into his parent's driveway, Garney spotted the yellow Volkswagen. What a coincidence, he thought, and from West Virginia as well. "Impossible," he said to himself. Garney gathered up his faithful pet, Wedgy, and walked to the house.

As he entered the kitchen and set his pet down, he said, "I'm back. Where's Bo?"

Bo replied from the family room, "In here, come and meet Madison."

Garney entered the family room to join the gathering, and Bo crossed the room to hug him. Garney only had a partial view of Madison as Bo blocked his line of sight while greeting his brother. Garney had a tightening of his stomach as he thought it couldn't possibly be her.

Her full view came into sight, and he yelled out, "NOOOOO damn it, no." Garney turned and fled from the room, followed quickly by Maggie and Wedgy. What had just occurred, thought the rest of his family. Madison knew. It was shattering and disturbing to her. It was not going to her zany plan.

Garney said to his mother, "Get her out of here. I will explain later. If someone doesn't tell her to get out of this house, I will physically throw her out myself. She is an evil person, Mom."

Maggie said, "What, why, I don't understand. Why are you upset? Bo's girlfriend seems so nice."

Garney, who was starting to breathe more normally and was composing himself, said, "She is gone."

He strode angrily in the direction of the family room. He crossed the room and forcefully grabbed Frankie by the arm. He began to pull her towards the kitchen and the exit. Now totally confused, Bo rushed to her defense and grabbed Garney, trying to pull him away. Instantaneously, Stephen joined the fray and tried to separate his two sons. Madison Frankie or Connie was spent sprawling to the floor and yelled, "But I love you, Garney. We are meant for each other. You have to love me. I know you do."

Everyone froze, and Bo shouted, "What the fuck."

Maggie sharply responded, "Bob, don't use that type of language. It is uncalled for."

Frankie, Maddy, or Connie started to try to begin to explain to the Fosters. It was not comprehended by any of the Fosters other than Garney, who grasped part of her rant. It was a jumble of what she had been doing. Five minutes later, nobody was much more aware of the situation when she finished. Total confusion reigned.

Stephen Senior stoically said, "Miss, I would like you to leave our home. This is complete confusion, and our family is going to try to sort it out. I may have to apologize to you later, but for now, you are not welcome here."

Bo quickly said, "Well, I am going to leave too. And Maddy, you have to explain to me what the hell is going on." Frankie quickly told Garney directly, "You have to come with me. We are meant to be together. Bo, I am sorry. You are a terrific guy, but Garney and I are meant for each other."

Garney and Bo said almost in unison, "Get the hell out of here."

Bo was so angry that he picked up her suitcase in the kitchen, stepped outside, and flung it with all his strength as far as he could. If there were an event for suitcase toss in the Olympics, his throw probably would have shattered the world record. The disturbed young woman finally stormed to her car, parting with a volley of threats. Leaving her suitcase where it lay, she entered her car and shouted they would all pay for this. She would destroy them as a family.

"Fucking Fosters, you will regret this, and Garney, you will be first," she screamed as she turned her key in the ignition.

"Bo, you blockhead will be next. You won't be able to sleep at night. Garney, you couldn't see what was good for you."

As the Volkswagen exited the driveway, Maggie started to sob, and Stephen wrapped his arms around his wife. He was trying to assure her that everything would be all right. The family moved together, returning to the security inside their home. Once inside, they all retreated to the family room.

Stephen began by stating, "This has sideswiped your mother and me, and I have no earthly idea what just occurred. For that matter, we have no idea what led up to this mad scene. It seems each of you boys can fill us in on your side of the story. Please enlighten us. Who wants to go first?"

The two sons stared at each other. They both stated that they would like to begin.

Garney said, "I think it all began with me, so please let me start."

Stephen said, "If it's okay with Bo, Garney, you may begin." Bo nodded in agreement. It gave him more time to gather the courage to explain to his mom, in particular, that they had been living together, a common practice among young couples these days. Garney began to relate his tale, beginning with the meeting on the first day at a restaurant in Raleigh. He referred to her as Connie initially, and he was advised later by other players on the tour that her name was Frankie. He revealed that she was stalking him at various events on the tour. She was initially a nuisance, and then she became frightening.

His constant rebuffing of her advances did not deter her insanity. Occasionally, he was interrupted by his mother, wondering why he didn't return home or call them to let them know what was going on. When Garney arrived at the part where Tom was tripped and injured, Maggie squeezed Stephen's arm. Garney omitted some events so as not to alarm and terrify his mother. The snakes were never mentioned. He felt his explanation was descriptive enough that some things could be eliminated. There was no point in relating that she slept undetected in the extra bed in Tom's room. In about an hour, Garney, with a few interruptions, was able to describe in some detail his adventures and misadventures. Maggie interrupted a few times. Stephen sat stoically pondering his son's adventure. Bo said nothing but shook his head from side to side with anger at times.

"You have had a terrible experience, Garney, and I am sure there is more to come out. It seems like a police matter. We would like to hear how Bo became involved; everything seems quite devious on her part. Until there is some resolution, Garney, it would appear that you should forgo the balance of the golf tour."

Garney began to protest, and his father, Stephen, said, "Let me finish. Bo, you start with your side of the story."

Bo's saga was not nearly as long. He was able to describe his events in about half an hour. He carefully omitted that they shared a motel room. Maggie interrupted to make sure Madison hadn't been affecting his grades. At one time, any excuse was enough to have Bob fall off the academic wagon. The young woman was now known by three names: Connie, Frankie, and Maddison. Who the hell was she?

Stephen stated, "I am going to contact the police department and see what Harv has to say about this. The two of you had better be available as he will probably have more questions. There may be enough for charges of some sort that can be laid. She may be wanted for questioning in that other state that Garney mentioned. Everyone, please let's relax; this will pass. Thus far, it has been a bad and uncomfortable scene which I hope can, in time, be put in the past. Now let's go out for a nice lunch; your mother needs a break after this kerfuffle. I will call Harvey from the restaurant."

The four, two parents and two sons, then departed for the favorite family restaurant, which was located on the main street in Grayling. This was usually Maggie's first choice for a restaurant to have a family brunch. As they were about to leave, Bo jammed her suitcase's contents back into the broken suitcase. A little later, he flung it again from the moving vehicle into a ditch in route to town.

# Chapter 63: Frankie Makes Her Plans

Frankie had left the Foster's driveway a little more than about two and a half hours ago. She believed all was not lost. This problem could be solved. All that was necessary for her was to create a change of plan. A little more violence was the answer: get their attention. First things first, get rid of the yellow Volkswagen and rent another car. A car that was very plain, very non-descriptive from a rental agency, probably a suburban vehicle. She could arrange to leave her car at the back of a lot or, better still, take it to a paint shop. She always hated the yellow color anyway. Now, it was too obvious for any of her plans. Maybe that was it. Garney didn't like the color of her car. Her thought sequences were scattered. They were becoming even more rambled and bizarre. He wouldn't be first on her list after all. Maybe Bo.

She needed to stay in the area, but staying in Grayling was too obvious for her; she would be too easily recognized. Checking her laptop for maps, Frankie decided that Traverse City, with a population of about 15,000, would be ideal. There were ample motels and enough people to blend in with, and as a tourist, there would be many other strange faces around. Surely, they would have an auto paint shop to change the color of her car. This would be her home base while she evened the score with the Foster family. The commute was merely fifty miles on state Highway seventy-two. Frankie began her drive on the highway in the direction of Traverse City. There would be clothing shops there to purchase a couple of new outfits, some toiletries, a new suitcase, and other necessities. Lots of restaurants and services. Certainly, it would have a gun shop or a hardware store to buy some more ammunition for her eight-shot Ruger handgun. She had her work cut out so that she could put her plan in motion.

# Chapter 64: Harvey Has Questions

The Foster family entered the Main Street restaurant and was greeted by Luci, a waitress who had worked there for over twenty years. Luci led them to a table, handed them menus, and described the day's specials.

Stephen asked for a table closer to the rear of the restaurant where there were no other customers, and Luci obliged, leading them to a more private area.

Luci turned to Garney and said, "What are you doing here? I thought you out being a golf player."

"I am having a week off, and it will give the other golfers a chance for some of the prize money with me not being there." Garney joked.

The waitress chuckled and said, "Well, mister moneybags, aren't you considerate? I'll give you people some time to look at the menu and be right back."

Lunch decisions were made quickly. When Luci returned to their table, they gave her their orders and choices.

When left alone in a quiet section of the restaurant, the conversation about their problem continued. Additional information was divulged, and possible solutions were tendered.

If nothing else, when their food arrived, it gave them a respite from the dilemma as attention was turned to their meals. After finishing his lunch, Stephen left the table and went to the counter to pay their bill. He then exited the eatery, and Maggie could see him outside on his cell phone. Stephen had called and was talking to his friend, hockey colleague, and state trooper Harvey Guidry.

A few minutes later, Stephen re-entered the restaurant and stated, "Harv will be coming to our house in about an hour. Does anybody have anything else that they want to do while we are downtown?"

No one seemed interested in anything but getting back to the safety of home.

About an hour and a half later, a state police car pulled into their driveway. Harvey exited his vehicle and, while approaching the house, noticed a small amount of clothing near the mouth of the driveway. He pondered, "What was the story behind that."

Stephen met him as he arrived at the door and said to Harv, "Come on in."

Harvey said hello to Maggie as she entered the kitchen to welcome him.

"Let's go to the den and talk with the boys, and we will try to fill you in on what we know," stated Stephen. The three adults were soon seated with the two Foster brothers. Harvey took out his notepad and a pen.

The officer said, "Let's start at the beginning. Tell me what happened and include all the details. First, though, what is with that few bits of clothing at the mouth of the driveway? Was it placed there by her? Did she leave it in that place? I want to make sure it is safe to handle?"

Bo sheepishly stated he had thrown it there in anger and that it did belong to her. He said that he threw the suitcase with most of her other stuff in it into a ditch on the way into town. Bo offered to pick the trash up and put it in a garbage bin later.

"Where did you throw it from originally?" questioned Harvey. Bo answered, "The doorway."

Harvey whistled and stated, "You could get a job as a bellhop. I am going to pick it up and put it in the squad car. It could be evidence. I'll be right back." With that, the officer left the room and then returned in about five minutes. Upon his return, he said, "Let's resume, or should I say start."

The following hour was a repeat performance of the family discussion earlier in the day. Guidry asked questions, and Bo and Garney answered them as best they could. Garney and Bo revealed as much as possible in front of their parents.

However, this time, the youngest son divulged the story of the snakes. Garney also indicated which police departments had been involved and informed Harvey of her stalking, vandalism, and the injury to Tom. After receiving a description of the yellow car and the suspect and writing several pages of their testimonies, Harvey finished the questioning and said his goodbyes. He then returned to the police station. He felt that the possibility of fingerprints on the suitcase might be of some value as the investigation unfolded. He thought there may or may not be a case or any charges at all. Time will tell.

# Chapter 65: Frankie's Agenda

Upon arriving in Traverse City, Frankie began first by seeking accommodation. After a drive about the motel strip, she settled on a two-story hotel that gave her a good view of the parking lot and the entrance to her hotel. She was also interested in being within walking distance of the main shopping area. Upon settling in her suite, Frankie began leafing through the telephone book's yellow pages, seeking an auto paint shop. Within ten minutes, she had located precisely what she needed. This company would even pick the car up and deliver it after the painting and drying were completed in about two or three days. Next on the agenda was the need for a rental car. Within half an hour, a rental car company was located and contacted. Once again, drop off and pick up were part of the package. A grey 4X4 suburban, a neutral-appearing vehicle, was chosen.

They would deliver the vehicle within the hour. After these transactions were completed, a trip to the local shopping area would follow. She needed a couple of changes of clothing and some toiletries. In the interim, while waiting for the vehicle, Frankie stretched out on the bed and thought of Garney. How could she win him over? She was prepared to be violent, which would seem to her to be the most sensible plan of attack. Her dreams might take a few days to come together, but she had some ideas. Suddenly, Frankie realized that she had a handgun under the backseat of the Volkswagen and that it might be needed. She certainly didn't want it discovered by the paint shop. Frankie quickly left her room for the parking lot and, just in time, removed the gun and placed it in her skirt pocket. No sooner had she returned to her room than her room phone rang. It was a call from the front desk to advise her that someone was there about her car. They were there to take the Volkswagen for painting. After Frankie dealt with the paint company and opted for an ash gray color for her Volkswagen, she walked him to the car. She found the paint shop owner quite comical as he drove away. He was, it seemed, nearly seven feet tall, and his knees were up to his chin as he left to drive back to the shop in the small vehicle. She always thought Bo looked funny in her little car. This guy won, hands down.

She returned to her room. In about another half an hour, the rental vehicle was delivered, and she was now free to take the short walk to the downtown shopping area. Three hours later, she returned to her room and was satisfied that all missions were accomplished. Frankie had acquired a different vehicle. She bought some new clothes at a Walmart, including some black garments to wear at night. A black balaclava, a black leotard, and a black sweatshirt. She had also recovered her handgun and ammunition just in case it was needed. Now, all that was left was to purchase more ammunition. Frankie located a store named "Guns n Bibles" in the Yellow Pages, which she found humorous. After a short trip, she returned to her room with her ammunition purchase and some takeout food she had bought at a drive-thru fast-food restaurant.

Frankie sat at the bedside desk and started making notes to establish plans for revenge on the Fosters. She had prepared a draft in about an hour, and several pages were balled up and thrown in the waste basket—a step-by-step course of action. Step one would begin tomorrow night. Darkness was necessary for her treachery against the Fosters. She remembered Bo telling her about the family cat. It was a birder. When the cat was let outside in the late evenings, she often proudly returned to the house with a field mouse or small bird in its mouth. Maggie would not let Wedgy in the house until someone removed the mouse or bird from the cat's mouth. Frankie never let on; she even knew the cat's name was Wedgy. This was possibly the first part of her plan.

# Chapter 66: Garney And George

The Foster family was up and around early the next morning. Stephen asked Bo to join him at the store that day. After breakfast, the two departed for the family hardware store. When his youngest son volunteered to join them and help out, Stephen quietly asked Garney to stay home to be with his mother. Stephen felt safer if someone was with Maggie. He still was not sure what they were dealing with or what that disturbed woman was capable of doing. The day turned out to be uneventful at both the store and their home. Maggie did receive a phone call from the police. Harvey wanted to know if there had been any further contact with Frankie, as this was the name he referred to the suspect.

He also indicated he had been in touch with the other state police agencies and was brought up to date on their reports. All of the various departments contacted were concerned that she may be dangerous. There was an all-points bulletin describing her yellow vehicle with West Virginia plates. The APB also requested police personnel to stop and question the vehicle operator but to approach with caution. A vague description of the suspect was included in the all-points bulletin. Garney hoped to visit Mr. Trent and other staff members that day but remained at home to ensure his mother was safe. Harvey did indicate that Michigan State troopers had checked the Ypsilanti motel where she had been staying and were doing an occasional drive-by.

Maggie and Garney had some wonderful talks that day about the positive side of the golf tour. He couldn't express enough how enjoyable most of the tour had been. She noticed how mature he seemed now after being out on his own for five years. Four years of college and almost a year on the golf tour. She was proud of her sons. Maggie thought to herself, where has the time gone? It seemed like yesterday that the three boys were roughhousing in the yard. They discussed his return to the tour, which was his initial plan. Like any other loving mother, Maggie was entirely set against him, flying back to return to Knoxville. Garney rejoining his friends, and the mini tour would probably not happen under the present conditions. Garney's rebuttals were weak, and it didn't look promising for his scheduled return to the tour. There had to be a resolution to this stalking situation before his going back would occur, and he could rejoin his two amigos. Bo would return to his classes on Saturday or Sunday, but Garney would not fly to Knoxville.

Bo returned from the hardware store in the early afternoon while his father remained to work with the remaining staff.

Garney was now free to visit Mr. Trent and the other staff at the country club. Twenty minutes later, Garney was in route to Birch Run for a visit. Immediately on arrival, he headed for Mr. Trent's office in the pro shop. George was pleased to have some time for some questions and answers with his protégé.

"How was your time on the tour so far, Garney? We read on the internet you have had some pretty good results." This level of golf tour did not receive any newspaper media attention in the local Michigan newspapers.

Garney was evasive about his dealings with Frankie. He did discuss the three amigos, their travels, and the golf tournaments. The agreement with Dale and Tom on prize sharing and the extra bedroom each week. Garney indicated that their sponsorships and winnings allowed them to live comfortably. None of the money worries that some of the other mini-tour golfers struggled with.

"When do you have to head back to the tour, Garney, probably on the weekend?"

Garney said, "Something has come up, and I am unsure if I can return right away."

"What's the problem, Garney? Is there anything I can do? It doesn't appear that you are short of money. Your game appears to be in good shape."

Garney did not want to deceive his friend, so he revealed the story in some detail. He included information from the beginning to the blowup at their home last night: "Mom thought she remembered seeing Frankie at the club earlier this summer. George, please keep this information to yourself."

George was stunned; he was finally George, and the news was disturbing. Garney was finally referring to him by his first name.

Garney had become an adult. George asked Garney, "Are the police involved?"

The young man replied that his father had contacted them, and Harvey Guidry had visited the house and was working on it as a case. George asked, "Can you describe her, Garney? Just a gut feeling, but I believe she may have been here for lunch recently."

After a description of Frankie, George was certain she had eaten lunch at 'The End Of The Run.' "I will keep an eye out for her if she ever returns here."

Garney excused himself and asked where Ben might be found. He wanted to say hello before returning home.

George said, "He is probably in the cart barns repairing something or some machinery."

They said their goodbyes, and Garney walked towards the cart barns for a brief visit with Ben before he headed home. Ben was delighted that Garney had stopped by for a visit.

"Looking for a greenskeeper job? I have an opening," said Ben jokingly.

Garney responded, "I have a four-year degree in grass cutting from Western Michigan, but I feel I am underqualified," as Garney teased him back.

The two bantered and talked about how things were going with each other. About twenty minutes later, Garney excused himself and headed home. As he drove while returning home, Garney hoped that the authorities had already arrested Frankie and that it could be over.

# Chapter 67: Property Damage

Frankie made a decision; she decided that the cat would wait. She would put the second part of the plan into action first. She left her motel and headed to a local restaurant for dinner. After a pleasant meal, Frankie returned to her hotel, changed into her newly purchased black outfit, and waited for darkness. She began her drive from Traverse City to Grayling in her rental suburban. An hour later, under darkness, she was nearing the Foster household. Plan B was about to occur. Maggie had a green thumb and worked diligently to keep beautiful flower and vegetable gardens. Her flower gardens were her pride and joy. On arriving at the Fosters, Frankie realized that she had reached her destination too early. Lights were still on in several locations in the Foster household.

She would find a quiet spot nearby to park and bide her time. About an hour and a half later, another drive past the Foster home, all the interior lights were out, and the house was in total darkness. Frankie doused her car headlights and slowly drove up the driveway into the Foster backyard. There was no reaction from the house. She slipped the vehicle into four-wheel drive and hit the accelerator. The wheels spun, and Frankie drove through every garden in her path. Flowers and vegetables alike were crushed, and deep ruts made the gardens unrecognizable as gardens. Frankie then sped to the front of the house and quickly did two giant donuts on the front lawn. Suddenly, a light was turned on upstairs. One more quick spin through the last beautiful flower garden on the front lawn before exiting the way she had entered. Frankie then sped off toward Traverse City and the safety of her motel room.

Before returning directly to her motel, the obsessed young lady drove the vehicle to a car wash in Traverse City, which she had identified earlier. She wanted to remove any evidence that was on the vehicle. Fifteen minutes later, the suburban looked brand new, and she returned to the motel. Step one was a success.

# Chapter 68: Viewing The Damage

The clamor outside their house was alarming and confusing. What the hell was going on outside? Bo was the first one down the stairs and to the kitchen door. He arrived in time to see taillights turning onto the road from their driveway. He thought, "What the fuck was that."

He turned on the outside light, which was not much aid in illuminating little more than the porch area. He was still unaware of all the damage to the property that had occurred. About this time, the remaining Fosters were arriving to join him, and Stephen asked, "What is going on, Bo?"

Bo responded, "I don't know. I saw tail lights leaving the driveway."

As she arrived, Maggie asked, "What was all the noise?"

Garney responded, "Whatever it was, it's not hard to guess who was behind this. I tell you, she's nuts. You never know what she is going to attempt."

"Let me get a flashlight," Stephen stated as he headed off to retrieve one from a drawer in the kitchen. When he returned with a large flashlight, Stephen and his sons exited the kitchen door and immediately saw that the front lawn had been destroyed.

Using the flashlight, Stephen scanned the large front lawn and saw that the sod was overturned in huge ruts making it unrecognizable as a lawn. Stephen, with a mild oath, said, "Damn, who is crazy enough to do something like this, and why? It is just sheer pettiness and destruction."

Garney said, "I am positive that it's her. This is the kind of stuff she is capable of doing. Unfortunately, it also means she is likely still in the area."

They returned to the house, and Bo told Maggie, "Mom, she ruined our front lawn. It was probably Madison or, sorry, Frankie, I should say. As Garney said, she is nuts, and I believe him. She is a wacko." He then recalled that he had been living with her and had slept with her. She was good for something.

"There is no point in calling the police at this hour. We will deal with this in the morning. Property damage is not likely a priority at this time of night." said Stephen.

The family was not yet aware of all the ruin that had occurred behind the house. The following day, the full extent of the destruction became evident. Maggie felt sick as she examined what was left of her gardens. All that work and care was destroyed in five minutes because of someone's sheer stupidity and vindictiveness.

Stephen called the police station and asked for his buddy Harvey Guidry. He was transferred to Harvey's desk almost immediately. Stephen told Harv that, more than likely, it was related to the stalking case they had been dealing with—the craziness that had happened earlier. He described how they were awakened last night and added what they awoke to this morning. The yard had been destroyed—front and back. Maggie's gardening and beautiful flower gardens are in ruins. The lawn was not recognizable.

Harvey stated he would be there shortly, and they ended their conversation.

The officer arrived half an hour later and examined the damage. He asked a few questions, and only Bo could offer him anything. He saw tail lights, but that was not much help. Harv wanted to know if they were Volkswagen tail lights. Bo could only offer they would have been higher and bigger than a Volkswagen, and he was sure they were not Volkswagen's tail lights.

Harvey said, "Well, we know two things: she is likely still in the area and probably has a different car. There is not much to go on, but you should consider some motion-activated outside lights."

Stephen said, "A neighbor down the road had some installed, but he had disconnected them. The wildlife, rabbits, skunks, and occasional deer were constantly setting them off by moving around his property during the night."

Harv responded, "Swamp, was your neighbor being stalked or harassed?"

"Point is well taken, Harv. I'll investigate installing some. We have a plentiful supply on stock in the store."

Harvey added, "We will keep our eye out and check some of the local motels for any sign of someone who fits her description. I'll see you later."

Stephen said, "Thanks, Harv, for all your help." as his friend was departing.

"It's my job, Swamp," replied his good friend.

The family, deeply concerned and frustrated by the blatant damage, returned to the house and gathered together in the family room. They discussed the situation and tried to come up with a solution to their problem. Frankie seemed to be in control, and the ball was in her court. She was in charge, and they wondered what could be done to reverse this horrible situation. Nobody had any answers. It was hoped the police could arrest and charge her, deterring any further vandalism or, even worse, an injury to a family member. They wanted to return to what had been their everyday normal lives.

# Chapter 69: Frankie And Wedge

Another day passed, and Frankie continued to work on her devious plans, trying to fine-tune them. She was still figuring out how to go about implementing what was her original step. She knew how much the cat meant to Garney. Frankie knew that Wedgy was left outside for about an hour or so late most evenings before the family retired for the night. Frankie needed something to attract the cat to her during that period. Frankie decided to purchase a small salmon steak from a local grocery store. Frankie was going to steal Wedgy. Once again, she donned the new outfit she had purchased: her black sweater, black leotard pants, and a black balaclava. The clothing worked very well in the darkness. Frankie would park a short distance away, walk to the Foster property, and lure Wedgy to her. If successful, Wedgy would be with her in Traverse City that night. Garney, hopefully, would be devastated. Wedgy would be missing. She could inform him by email that Wedgy was in good hands, and they could work something out together if he wanted to see his cat again.

By eleven o'clock, Frankie and Wedgy were safely in her motel room. The plan had worked to perfection, and now she was certain the Foster family were searching for their pet. Frankie did not want to get too attached to the cat in the event that the next part of her plan failed. The second part of the plan was distasteful even to her. It might, unfortunately, be necessary. Frankie sat at the desk and typed an email to Garney on her laptop. She explained the situation to him. She hit send.

Back at Garney's home, the entire family was outside calling Wedgy's name as they spread out and scoured their property. The family heard Bo cursing as he tripped on a furrow in the lawn. Maggie reminded him not to use that language. Garney felt certain that Frankie was somehow involved in Wedgy's disappearance. His emotions ran from being frightened to being furious. He hoped that his pet Wedgy would suddenly appear proudly carrying a field mouse in her mouth. After an hour of searching, the family returned to the house.

Maggie said, "We can check through the night to see if Wedgy has returned." Garney knew with his inner feelings that it was likely hopeless. The bitch had taken her or done something with her. He raged silently and rechecked the kitchen door for Wedge before retiring to his bedroom.

The next morning, there was still no sign of his pet. Garney and other family members had checked the kitchen door through the night for any signs of Wedgy wanting to enter the house. While eating breakfast, Garney opened his computer tablet to check his email. He was hoping to hear from Dale or Tom, and he found Frankie's note.

He quickly called for anyone who could hear, "I told you. She has Wedgy, damn, damn, damn. She is the efin worst person on the face of this earth, the worst person on the face of the earth. I'd like to choke her. Where the hell is she? How can she do this? Why is she doing this to me?"

The rest of the family had arrived in the kitchen and were trying to console Garney. Stephen said, "Garney, we will get to the bottom of this. We will get Wedgy back and put an end to her vindictive shenanigans. I am going to phone Harv and tell him her latest prank. I will ask if they have the ability and technology to trace this email."

Graney replied, "Thanks, Dad, I just can't see what we can do. She seems to hold most, if not all, of the cards. It seems that she won't stop until I become her boyfriend, which is the last thing I will ever do. This is the first crazy person I've ever met."

Stephen said, "I'm going to call Harv. If there is anything new, I will let you know."

When he returned, Stephen relayed his officer friend's update: "Harv said that there is nothing new. He visited most of the motels and hotels in town with her description and came up with nothing. There have been no sightings of a yellow Volkswagen in the area. He felt she was like a ghost. He has called and been in touch with other local detachments, and they are keeping an eye out for the car. Not much good news, but that's what they have. A missing cat is not at the top of the priority list. Nor is what they referred to as a jilted girlfriend. Our department is presently having a gun standoff with a rural area homeowner, and there was a fatal automobile accident on the highway north of here. These two incidents took up a lot of the workforce. Harvey said, "We need a break, a phone call, or a sighting of the girl. Anything."

The rest of the day passed with no new developments. No Frankie, no Wedgy, no yellow Volkswagen. Stephen spent the afternoon dealing with local contractors and landscapers to try and obtain quotes for yard repair work. He also contacted their insurance company to file a claim and to check and see what coverage their policy contained. Bo spent the day at the hardware store filling in for his father as store manager. During the afternoon, Garney emailed back and forth with Dale and Tom, explaining what had gone on in Grayling and informing them his return was up in the air. He might not be back this year; he might not miss a week. He might be back for the last two weeks of the schedule. Tom and Dale guessed correctly that it had something to do with Frankie, and it was getting serious and dangerous. Both felt relieved that Garnet wouldn't be joining them, as neither wanted to be in the crossfire as peripheral damage. They hadn't suspected it had become as serious as it had become. This situation had to be sorted out first.

# Chapter 70: Wedge And The Shed

The evening arrived, and plans were being made simultaneously in Grayling and Traverse City.

The Fosters were discussing the possibility of Garney missing the rest of the golf tour. Garney's position was that he might need more points for entry to the Korn Ferry tour next year. His parents were understandably more concerned about his safety than his points. Bo wanted to talk about his return to Ypsilanti this coming weekend. Garney said he would have to cancel his plane ticket if he could not return to Winston-Salem for the tour. He offered to drive Bo back to college if he was still here at home. In their discussion, they all hoped that Frankie's vandalism would end and things would return to normal. That she would return Wedgy safely.

In Traverse City, Frankie was working on her next step of winning over Garney. They needed to become a couple. She was also concerned that now, being wanted and a fugitive, protecting herself was more important than it had ever been before. She determined that it was best to carry her handgun and some of the extra ammunition on her night outings.

Later that night, she gathered up Wedgy and began a trip that even to her seemed evil. She remembered bringing the handgun and a large knife she had purchased earlier that afternoon. It was two in the morning when she arrived at her favorite parking spot a short distance from the Foster home. Frankie removed Wedgy from the car. Using the long knife before she changed her mind, she violently stabbed Wedgy several times until there was no further motion from the pet. Dressed in black, carrying the lifeless Wedgy, she silently moved along the edge of the yard to the garden shed. Frankie impaled the dead cat to the door when she reached the shed. Leaving as stealthily as she had arrived, Frankie set out on her drive to return to Traverse City. Her destruction had escalated.

The following morning, Maggie was enjoying her coffee in the breakfast nook when something caught her eye on the garden shed door. What is that? She pondered. Bo came downstairs, poured himself a coffee, joined his mother, and said, "Good morning, Mom."

Maggie asked, "Bob, what is that on the shed door? I can't quite make it out."

Bo squinted and said to his mother, "I can't make it out either. I don't know, I'll take a look. It's probably nothing."

Bo slipped on some shoes, opened the door, and began to walk to the back of the yard. As he walked, he was disgusted at the state of the yard. It looked like a war zone. Turning his attention to the shed as he approached, he clasped his hands to his face and nearly fell to his knees. It was Wedge, no, no, no, what do I do? Bo quickly decided that he did not want Garney nor his mother to see the family pet this way and carefully removed the cat. He laid the cat behind the shed and wondered if he should bury Wedgy. The shovels were right there in the shed. Bo buried his head in his arms as he leaned against the shed and then decided to return to the house. Perhaps Garney wanted to see Wedgy one last time. Bo entered the kitchen with tears in his eyes.

Garney was sitting with their mother, and as Bo approached the two of them, he could hardly speak.

Bo finally said, "That fucking asshole killed Wedgy. She stuck him to the shed door. I'll kill her. She wants to hope the police find her before I do."

For the first time in her life, at least the first time to any of her son's knowledge, Maggie swore, saying, "Bob, you are right. She is a fucking asshole."

Garney had buried his face in his hands and was sobbing. Tears were streaming down Maggie's face as she began to cry. Stephen walked in to see his family crying and sobbing. Even Bo had tears on his cheeks.

Stephen asked, "What's going on? What happened? Is Stephen Junior all right?"

Garney leaped to his feet and said, "Where is she? I want to see her."

Bo told Garney, "I'll take you there in a bit."

Stephen repeated, "What in the hell is going on."

Maggie tried to explain to Stephen what had happened to their pet Wedge.

Stephen said, "Garney, I am so sorry, son; we are going to have to take more precautions on our end until this woman is caught. She is dangerous and has no moral or ethical values. I am going to call Harv. Everyone remains here."

Stephen left to make the phone call and returned shortly. "Harvey said he would be out as soon as possible, and he was leaving the station immediately."

Bo and Garney left the house and headed for the garden shed. They were gone for about an hour. As they returned, they could see a squad car in the driveway. Entering the family room, Bo said they found a nice spot in the woods and had buried Wedge. Bo had brought the knife back, which he had wrapped in a piece of paper in case there were any fingerprints.

Harvey and their mother and father were discussing the events. They had told the officer that the boys, especially Bo, might have something to add. Bo had been the first on the scene. Harvey complimented Bo on his insight in protecting the knife for fingerprints. It seemed that night after night, Frankie had done something criminal to the Fosters and their property without missing a night. Harv suspected that more evil might be and was probably coming.

# Chapter 71: A Break in The Case

Later that morning, back in Traverse City, Frankie received a phone call from the paint shop that her car was ready and that he could deliver it to the motel. He was looking for a time frame for delivery. Frankie asked him to give her a couple more hours. She had slept late due to her night prowling and was very tired. In the meantime, she called the rental car company and arranged to return their vehicle in a few more days. Frankie went back to bed.

Finally, a break, and it was a fluke. The owner of the local automotive paint shop, whose nickname was Kong, was six feet eight if he was an inch tall, and he had some time to kill. He had an hour or so before delivering the car to Frankie at the motel. Kong decided to grab a coffee at one of the local main street restaurants. It was a favorite spot for many of the residents to grab their morning coffee. There was always a group of about ten retired senior citizens, men who were referred to by other locals as the Town Senators in attendance. When Kong entered the restaurant, he spotted his neighbor Jeff, a state trooper who was having coffee with a fellow officer. The trooper waved him over to join them at their table. He gave the waitress his order as he was striding over to join them at their booth, a large double-double. After an introduction to the other officer, they began to chat about the local high school's football team's chances that fall. The team was ranked relatively high in the state during the preseason rankings. Conversations came and went.

Near the end of their session, Kong stated, "The funniest thing was this broad asked me to paint her car. There was nothing wrong with it, and I did it, and I'm delivering it today. Who am I to turn down the money?"

The officers' ears perked up, and one asked, "What kind of car is it?"

Kong said, "It was a yellow Volkswagen, and I painted it an ash gray."

Jeff, his neighbor, quickly asked, "Where does she live?"

Kong replied, "She doesn't live here in town; she's staying at the motel just past the box stores out in the west end. Did she do something wrong?"

The other officer told Kong, "Don't mention that you were talking to us when you deliver the vehicle. It's probably nothing. We don't want to spook or upset her if it is something important."

The tab came, and Kong took the bill and jokingly said, "I got it, no traffic tickets, okay."

They exited the restaurant and went their separate ways. The police officers agreed to meet at the local detachment. A short while later, they discussed their information with their desk sergeant. The desk sergeant contacted the Grayling detachment and advised them of a possible connection with their case. It was decided to put surveillance on the now gray Volkswagen located in the motel parking lot. They wanted to be certain it was their suspect; the officer would await her arrival at the car before approaching her. The Grayling station also decided that they would do some drive-byes of the Foster home regularly throughout the night for a few more nights.

# Chapter 72: The Fire and The Chase

Later that night, Frankie left her motel and exited the parking lot, driving the rental suburban. When she exited the motel, the officer in the unmarked car thought this might be her. However, this lady entered a gray suburban and drove away. In the rear compartment of the rental car was a full red plastic gas can—part of plan four. The undercover officer was replaced at about midnight by fresh troops. The gray Volkswagen remained in its parking spot. Frankie planned to burn down the Foster's garden shed when all was quiet. She was unaware that the Fosters country road she would be visiting was being patrolled with semi-regular visits by marked and unmarked police cars.

Two hours later, she was at her destination and prepared to add arson to her bevy of crimes. Once again, she parked off-road in her favorite spot a little distance from her target. Dressed in her all-black outfit, she was removing her gas can from the rear of the vehicle when headlights appeared, approaching her hiding spot on the rural road from her right. She quickly closed the hatch and ducked behind the car. She cursed the interior lights as the timer briefly kept them on when the doors closed. The interior lights finally went out just before the car passed. It appeared she was safe for now. This time, she removed the gas can in time when another vehicle appeared but traveling in the opposite direction. Again, the interior light shone and seemed to extinguish just in the nick of time. Luck was on her side.

She left her suburban vehicle while carrying the gas can and moved towards the Fosters' home and their garden shed. Frankie cursed herself as she had not accounted for the weight of the gas can, and her handgun was digging into her side, where she had tucked it into her leotard. Halfway there, another car was approaching, causing her to dart off the road into the tall grasses. Once the car had passed, Frankie continued on her path to the targeted garden shed. She wondered why there was so much traffic for this time of night.

When she arrived at the garden shed, she began to slosh gasoline on and around the building, trying to use all of the gasoline. A few minutes later, it was ablaze. Frankie was running as if her life depended on it to return to her car. She heard an explosion; it was likely the gas tank of the riding tractor. Frankie arrived at her vehicle and began to pull out of her spot when another car appeared about half a mile behind her. Frankie put her foot to the floor on the accelerator. Another vehicle was now coming toward her. Both vehicles had turned on their sirens and their flashing blue lights.

Frankie took dead aim at the police car coming at her, hoping that she would win this game of chicken. She guessed right as the squad car peeled off the road into the ditch and onto the shoulder. As she was speeding by the ditched police car, an officer fired three shots at her, all of which struck the suburban vehicle. She knew she had to lose these police officers, and her reckless driving kept her ahead of the two cars that were now pursuing her. Frankie was glad she had her handgun if she needed to use it. The extra cartridges were out of her reach in the rear of the vehicle and would be of no use to her. Poor organizational planning, she thought, was not like her. She was usually better prepared. She was now on the highway heading towards Traverse City, and the powerful squad cars were closing ground. Suddenly, there was a third car in the chase, then a fourth. Her GPS showed a sideroad ahead on the right. She turned onto the side road almost on two wheels and nearly overturned. In her haste to escape, she had not noticed the NO EXIT sign on the road she had just entered. Within approximately two miles, the road ended, and she came to a stop with gravel flying in all directions. All the police cars were close behind. Frankie was cornered. A megaphone asked her to exit the vehicle with her hands raised; this was not an option for her. It was not going to happen. She remembered that her extra ammunition was in the very rear of the vehicle, and unless she could access it, all she had was the eight bullets in her handgun. While she was deliberating her next move, some of the officers had left their squad cars and were moving through the undergrowth to surround her. Frankie had gone over the edge. She reached her arm out the window and fired a shot at the empty vehicle that had stopped directly behind her. Seven shots were left. She could hear sirens as reinforcements heading for the scene in the distance. She was not going to spend any of her time incarcerated in a woman's prison.

She continually screamed at the officers. Her latest shout, "I'm fucking going to take some of you with me." Frankie then rapidly fired five shots at the ever-increasing number of the State of Michigan vehicles. The empty squad car directly behind her car took the brunt of her volleys. Two cartridges left. Several times, the loud hailer asked her to throw out her gun and step out of the vehicle with her hands raised. The police were trying to keep her alive. Was she planning a suicide death by the cops? Suddenly, there were two more shots, and her abusive language stopped. Frankie was not going to be incarcerated. She was going to be interred. She had taken her own life.

Frankie had lived a life that had doom written all over it from a very young age. She had a difficult childhood without real caring parents. She hadn't developed any values or any discipline. She had caused pain for herself and others in her short twenty-something years. For the Fosters, the pain and fear were finally over. Connie's family was probably saddened but relieved.

# Chapter 73: The Aftermath

The Fosters stood together in their yard, watching the shed fully ablaze and burning to the ground. They heard two more explosions as the tires blew up inside the garden shed. Next, they could hear the volunteer fire department trucks approaching. Another night of terror that they had to face, thanks to a deranged Frankie. The tanker truck arrived first, followed by the fire engine and a few pickup trucks. Stephen asked the drivers to drive to the back as the lawn was already in ruins. Earlier, the family had heard what sounded like a few gunshots. Unbeknownst to them, it had been the start of the car chase. They wondered as a family what Frankie would possibly do next. Stephan intended to have the motion detector that he had brought home from the store installed. Bo recommended that he get the deer rifles out to have them handy if they were needed. Was she capable of burning down the house with people still sleeping in their beds? The crew was efficient, they were extremely well-practiced machines, and the flames were doused very quickly. There was next to nothing left of the garden shed. The only thing visible was the skeletal remains of the garden tractor.

Talking out loud, Stephen mused that a guard dog might be necessary. Maggie was near exhaustion and hanging on to Bo and Garney for support. The family thanked the firefighters for their assistance and the quick response to their emergency as the volunteers drove back up the driveway. Gerry, the volunteer fire chief, was driving a pickup truck, and his passenger, one of Stephen's antique hockey teammates, had stopped to talk to Stephen and expressed their condolences.

"When will it end?" asked Maggie.

With the fire brigade only just disappearing down the road, a vehicle entered the driveway, and fear enveloped the entire family. Was it her? They were collectively relieved to realize it was Harvey in his police cruiser. Harvey exited his vehicle and approached the Fosters.

As he neared the family, Harvey said, "It's all over. You have no more worries."

Garney responded enthusiastically, "Did you catch her."

Harv said, "I should not say this, but it's even better. She committed suicide, which is better for those she has hurt and better for her. Based on everything I have investigated and heard, I think the girl was a mess. Garney, we were looking into having your two roommates interviewed in case they could add anything. I will drop by tomorrow and give you all the details. You can rest easy tonight. I'll see you people tomorrow. Good night, all." With that, the trooper returned to his squad car and left for his detachment's office.

Stephen said, "Let's call it a day. We have work to do around here tomorrow and beyond. We can breathe again, but we have lots of work ahead of us and some decisions to be made." The family headed for the house and their beds.

# Chapter 74: Normalcy

The family arose the following day and met in the kitchen for hopefully a relaxing breakfast. Nobody had slept well; it was going to take time. They were all curious about Connie, Frankie, or Maddy. This would have to wait until Harvey visited. Garney wanted to know if he would be returning to the tour on Sunday. Things were safe now. Maggie was still hesitant to give her approval.

Stephen read her vibes quickly and said, "Give your mother and I a chance to discuss it further. You may need a bit of time to get over this. I recognize you are a grown man who can make his own decisions, but we would like some input in order to help you."

A few hours later, Harvey Guidry drove into their driveway. Syeve and a landscaper were in the yard assessing the property damage. Stephen excused himself, and then he and Harvey entered the residence. Maggie offered them both a cup of coffee. Harvey replied, "Yes, thank you, just black, thanks." After Maggie poured a cup for the officer, Stephen poured his coffee, and the group retired to the family room. In a somewhat detailed version, he explained what had transpired in sequence as the police were able to piece it together. Fortunately, Frankie had turned down a dead-end road, saving the police from chasing her into a populated area. She had recklessly fired her gun, and there were no citizens around to become peripheral damage.

"Our department had several drive-byes on your road in marked and unmarked cars, and this is where the chase began. I apologize for saying what I said about the result being better than a capture. She had her problems, but she was a human being. Maybe with help, she could have turned herself around. I guess I was just happy that my colleagues, my friend, and his family were unharmed and safe."

The Fosters thanked Harvey and the police force for everything they had done to protect them during this frightening ordeal.

As he was leaving, Harvey asked Garney, "Are you heading back on your golf tour right away?"

Garney responded, "I haven't decided yet, maybe in a week. I think I need a little more time. It would mean leaving in a couple of days, and I don't think I am ready yet."

With that, life began to return to normal for the Fosters.

The next day, by email and telephone, Garney contacted Dale and Tom and gave them a Readers Digest version of the happenings in Grayling.

He wrote I won't be able to join you in Winston, but I will join you in Statesville for that tournament and also the last one in Charlotte.

During the phone call, he described to his friends all the chronological happenings; all Dale could say was, "No shit, no shit." He sometimes had a way with words. They reported that Tom had fully recovered and was working out at the gym and running the sideroads near Bobcaygeon to prepare for his return to the golf tour. He had renewed his relationship with his high school sweetheart from the nearby small town of Fenelon Falls.

The week passed quite quickly. On Sunday, Garney drove Bo back to his classes at Eastern Michigan, which was a good bonding experience for both of them.

It seemed like it was no time, and Garney was soaring through the sky to resume what was his passion.

# Chapter 75: The Family Returns

Maggie and Stephen were almost empty nesters now. They always looked forward to having their sons come home for visits. It didn't remain that way for long, as Bo dropped out of college and returned to Grayling to work full-time in Foster's hardware store. It was still his vocation and his passion.

A few years later, Stephen Junior graduated from law school and opened a law practice in Grayling, mainly dealing with deeds, wills, and house closings. He and Jenny Marie, with their family, purchased a home in a small development on the outskirts of Grayling. Maggie now had two granddaughters. Finally, there were little girls to spoil and to care for occasionally.

After two more years of chasing his dream and not advancing past the Korn Ferry Tour, Garney returned to Grayling. George hired him as an assistant pro at the Birch Run Golf and Country Club. After a couple more years, Garney replaced George Trent as the head golf professional. George had retired to the Villages community in the southern state of Florida.

Garney's life was full, and he managed the golf club in the manner of his predecessor. On Saturdays, he would meet with the young golfers who participated in the youth program as he had when he was a junior. He would offer them guidance and minor adjustments in their game, just as George had taught him in his youth.

# Chapter 76: Garney and His Gal

Garney later had a pleasant surprise that changed his life. He learned that Carley and Nick were getting a divorce and going their separate ways. It was irreconcilable differences. Nick had moved with his newfound woman to the state of California. Nick learned to surf while in the Carolinas, which became his passion. His new love was a surf bunny, and they had moved to Ocean Beach near San Francisco for the bigger waves.

Carley Brophy chose to return to Grayling, where she was the happiest, and reinstated her realtor license. She was welcomed back into the community with open arms and prospered in the home sales business. Before long, she and Garney began to become an item. No longer were the prior clandestine meetings a method of seeing each other. The age difference was not a problem and they had moved in together within a year.

As the seasons passed, the Foster household became a place of laughter, support, and brotherly love. And in the quiet moments, Maggie was her happiest.

At their residence, in the evenings, Garney would often find Carley curled up at his side, a constant reminder of the bond they shared and the journey that lay ahead.

## Dear Reader,

Thank you for embarking on this literary journey with me. Your time and attention are invaluable, and I sincerely hope my book has left a lasting impression on you.

If you enjoyed the experience, I would be immensely grateful if you could take a few moments to share your thoughts by leaving an honest review on Amazon. Your feedback helps other readers discover the book and provides valuable insights for future works.

To submit a review, please follow these simple steps:

- Visit the book's page on Amazon.
- Scroll down to the "Customer Reviews" section.
- Click on the button that says, "Write a customer review."
- Rate the book and share your thoughts.

Your words carry great weight, and I truly appreciate the time you take to express your opinions. Whether you loved the story or have constructive feedback, your review contributes to the growth and improvement of my writing.

Thank you once again for being a part of this literary journey.I'm grateful for your support, and I look forward to reading your thoughts.

Warm regards,

**David Pendlebury**